Boulevard Books
New York

Copyright 2012 Avi Gvili

ISBN: 978-0-9829156-2-2

For Mazal and Lilo Gvili,

Friends and dear parents.

Introduction

From as far back as I can remember I loved reading stories. Whether it was the terrifying tales of the brothers Grimm or the magical ones of Hans Christian Anderson, stories were dear friends of my childhood. I was to learn later that the reason I liked them so much had to do with this central principle of Aesthetic Realism, the philosophy founded by American poet and educator, Eli Siegel: *All beauty is a making one of opposites, and the making one of opposites is what we are going after in ourselves.* I began to understand, for example, that while **The Elves and the Shoemaker** was a story that was *strange* and magical, it also had the *ordinary* emotions of people—the lovable shoemaker and his wife—as they worried about money, something I saw in my parents.

In college I discovered the great short story writers. I was thrilled the first time I read Guy De Maupassant's "The Necklace" and relished it again and again. Time has judged the story to be a great one, but why it is, is explained by Eli Siegel. "In the short story there is a feeling of point, which changes into something that takes on a wider and wider meaning."

Through this, for instance, I saw that a large aspect of the power of "The Necklace" lies in the tremendous point it comes to when Madame Loisel finds out she has spent many back breaking years working for nothing; yet, the meaning of how her vanity blinded her goes out, is true through the ages because we feel *related* to her. "The short story is supposed to have a point," Siegel explains, "and then is supposed to ripple out; in fact, we can imagine a good short story being like a stone thrown into a lake in 1906 and it's still rippling out..."

It was in consultations given at the Aesthetic Realism Foundation in Soho, NY that I was first encouraged to take the short story form seriously, and it was there that the art in me was encouraged. The purpose of writing, my consultants explained, was to say what was true, to be fair to reality outside myself. This was completely new to me, and for the first time, I felt I had a solid foundation upon which to begin writing.

In my late twenties I continued my study of Aesthetic Realism in professional classes with Ellen Reiss, critic, poet, and Chairman of Education. In these wide and culturally rich classes I began to understand that at the very heart of writing was how a person sees words representing the outside world. Learning that my job as a writer was to be exact about words standing for people, emotions, objects, and more, was a breakthrough for me, and for that I am very grateful.

That the short story has a *structure*—and is not, as the admirable John Updike describes it, "…a human endeavor that is in the end so subjective"[1]—is still blazingly new in the world of literature more than a half century after it was first explained.

In this collection I have tried to consciously write according to Siegel's principle of the short story, and in so doing, I have found it to be immeasurably valuable as an artistic guide. It is, I believe, the understanding long sought for by writers.

Avi Gvili, May 2012

---

1 The Best American Short Stories of the Century Ed. John Updike, NY, Boston; Houghton Mifflin Co. 1999 p. xii

CONTENTS

Prologue

"Hey, Jeremiah—how goes it today?"

"Pretty good, Harold."

"How can things be going good at the age of one hundred and ten? At that age the only thing that feels good is just wakin' up in the morning."

"Can't say as I agree with you, Harold. I wake up with good feelings, and that means a whole lot."

Jeremiah Jenkins picked up his Orange Juice, held it up to an imaginary audience and took a sip. "Ahh, that sure is tasty," he said, smiling at his friend Harold Ickes, who couldn't help but reciprocate the good cheer emanating from the lively centenarian seated across from him. The bright morning sun beamed down on the two elderly gentlemen sitting on the veranda of the New Horizons Senior Citizens Home. To their right, two lively women engaged in a vigorous card game.

"I GOT YOU NOW, MARGARET!

"THAT'S WHAT YOU THINK, EDITH!"

"Sam's not doin' so well," remarked Harold, nodding towards a man in a wheel chair on their left. A bathrobe hung loosely on his thin frame. His eyes were closed.

"Edith told me she overheard the doctor tell Ms. Barts that it was only a matter of days," Harold explained. "Such a shame. You should have seen him a year ago—ninety, and still full of spit and vinegar. His wife's death broke him." He let out a long sigh. "It happens to the best of us, I guess."

Silence filled the empty space that hung heavy between the usually talkative friends. Suddenly, Jeremiah looked up at the morning sky.

"Dang it, Jeremiah—why you always looking up at the heavens? You talkin' to God or somethin'?

"Somethin' like that," he said, a smile curling the edge of his lips. A moment later he stood up.

"Where you headed?" Harold asked.

"Not far," Jeremiah replied, stepping towards Sam Westerfield.

The bright Florida sun blazed in the morning sky as Jeremiah pulled up a chair next to his sleeping friend. "Sam," he whispered. "Sam, it's me. Jeremiah."

Slowly, Sam Westerfield opened his eyes.

"Jeremiah, that you?"

"Yes, Sam. It's me." Sam extended his hand. Jeremiah clasped it warmly. For a moment, the two sat in silence.

"Not long now," Sam whispered.

"Maybe, maybe not," Jeremiah replied. He looked up at the sky, slowly following an imaginary point across the heavens, until by degrees his gaze fell upon his tired friend. "Would you like to hear a story?"

Sam's eyebrows lifted. "A story—what about?"

"Life and love, and things like that."

"Sure…couldn't hurt," Sam replied, and raised his head

The Assassin

It was a year or so after college that Sebastian began to feel a need to be with a woman, a need that was different than what he had felt in the past. He was getting bored and felt that life was more interesting when he was with a woman steadily. So it was with this state of mind that he drove on the Long island Expressway on a breezy Saturday night, heading into Manhattan to meet his fraternity brothers at Geo, the new hot spot. He turned the volume on his car radio higher, blasting the new song by Dupri.

As the warm summer air rushed into his Audi Twin Turbo, he turned the music even higher. Suddenly, the Ford Explorer he was trailing darted to the right lane, revealing a traffic jam a half-mile long. He slammed on the brakes, skidding to a stop inches before he was to crash into the back of an old, brown Chevrolet Dart.

"Damn it!" he yelled, banging on the wheel in frustration. "WHAT THE HELL!" he shouted out the window. Anger, hot and crazed, surged up within his chest.

BEEEEEEEEEEP! BEEEEEEEEEP! He banged on his horn again and again. "'GET OUT OF THE WAY! He wanted to get out of the car and hurt the driver.

But he decided not to. He couldn't be doing things like that anymore, he thought as he turned up the volume once more.

Five minutes later he was speeding into the Queens Midtown Tunnel. A half-mile back, the scared face of a ten-year-old girl peered out of the window of a Chevy Dart.

"Keep it close," he barked to the valet twenty minutes later as he threw him the keys to the Audi.

Club GEO stood high and wide in front of him. Encompassing half a city block, it was a rectangular building, two stories high with no noticeable windows. A dark marble like stone covered the exterior. A line of twenty somethings snaked down the block. A dark haired woman primped and prodded with aloof sexuality.

Recognizing him immediately, the thick bouncer guarding the entrance motioned for Sebastian to enter. He winked at the large black man, threw a careless glance over his shoulder, and walked into the deafening wall of sound that met him in the shadowy foyer.

"Twenty dollars," the cashier declared a moment later.

"I'm comped," he replied. "Sebastian Fortane. It's taken care of."

She sniffed, and then checked the clipboard to her right. "Sorry. No Sebastian Fortane on the list."

"Check it again!"

"I checked it right the first time. You want in or what?"

"We got a problem here?" A dark skinned man emerged out of the shadows.

"Whatever," murmured Sebastian as he threw the cashier a twenty-dollar bill, and turned towards the ornate doors that signaled the entrance to the dance floor.

"Wait a minute—you need a stamp," the cashier cried.

"I don't do stamps," he called back. Two large men in dark suits with telephone wires wrapped around their ears flanked either side. One stepped forward and automatically patted Sebastian down. A minute later, he stepped in.

Immediately, laser like strobe lights accosted his vision. A stream of steady, pulsating beats blasted out of the ten-foot speakers that lined the wall. Sebastian scanned the crowd in a slow 180-degree gaze that finally landed on the mirrors located to the far right of him.

He thought about getting a drink, but decided against it. I gotta get in there first, he thought heading to a shadowy room in the far end of the dance floor.

A thin man in horn rimmed glasses and spiky hair stood guard over the VIP room, busily checking over a clipboard in his right hand.

"I'm here for Robert's party," Sebastian said casually.

"Name!"

"Sebastian Fortane."

The man scurried over the contents of the clipboard, running his index finger up and down, until having reached a satisfactory point, he pulled back the blood red curtains and stepped out of the way to allow entry.

Smoke, thick and opaque, slowly climbed up to the ceiling. In the rear by the glass encased DJ, a bartender poured three shots of a lime colored liqueur.

"Yo, over here!"

A tall man with wavy blond hair gestured from the bar. Sebastian recognized Robert Boidan and walked over.

"What up, kid?"

"Chillin," Sebastian replied, eyeing a red-haired girl standing ten steps behind Robert.

"It's been a long time. How you been?" Sebastian nodded at the bartender, and then pointed to Robert's drink.

"Jack Daniels and Coke," Robert declared.

"Can't go wrong with that—one of the quickest ways to get hammered," replied Sebastian.

"I hear that!"

"Ten dollars," the dark haired bartender demanded as he placed the molasses colored drink on the bar.

"He's with me," Robert stated. A nod, and the bartender rushed to take another order.

"That's not what they said at the front door."

"Listen, bro. I do what I can." Slowly, Robert stirred his drink. Sebastian nodded slightly as he scanned the room. A soulful crooner filled the air with longings of love and lust. A couple moved sensually towards each other in the center of the room.

In the two years since college, Sebastian had often thought about the time he spent being in the fraternity with Robert. Hazy memories of real and imagined experiences, much of it alcohol induced, crowded his mind.

There was the time he finally went out with Damaris Stevens only to end up drunk at the bar yelling at her for some reason he couldn't now remember. Her pained expression still haunted him.

Vaguely, he also felt there were so many people he did not get to know, experiences he did not have. Sebastian swore to himself he would never let opportunities pass him by again.

Yeah, he thought, looking around the large room full of people; this time it's gonna be different. Suddenly, two muscular arms grabbed him.

"Damn it!" Sebastian exclaimed, spilling his drink forward. Turning around, he saw Nick Grimaldi grinning at him.

"Still runnin' up on people, huh Nick," he said, wiping droplets of alcohol from his dark leather blazer. Anger flashed over his face as he turned to the bar to order another Jack and Coke.

"How you been?" asked Nick.

"You know…it's all good. Makin' some good cash as a broker with my dad's company."

"Heard about that." Nick rubbed his neck. His eyes darted nervously. "I've been thinking about real estate myself. Can't seem to get a job."

"I'm sorry to hear that," replied Sebastian, his eyes following the movements of the red head he had seen earlier.

They talked about college and what they've been doing in the two years since then. And in the time it took Sebastian to finish his drink they covered two years of life.

"Listen Nick, I need another drink. You want one?" Sebastian asked half-heartedly.

"Na, I'm good. Thanks." They shook hands and Sebastian turned to the bar.

"One more," he called out. A minute later, a fresh drink in his hand, Sebastian turned to examine the contents of the dance floor.

He was immediately attracted to the way she danced. Her body throbbed to the swift beats blasting out of the ten-foot speakers lining the wall.

She's young; barely twenty, Sebastian thought.

For some time, he explored her barely concealed body. His eyes ran over the curves and outlines of her form, drinking in the human capital. He shot back the remains of his drink, and began to strategize his approach.

Sebastian nodded to the bartender.

"What can I do you for?"

"A bottle of Moet, chilled with two glasses."

The bartender hesitated. "That's $150 a bottle."

Sebastian glared at him. "You got a problem with that?"

The bartender scuttled away, returning a few minutes later with two slim glasses and a bottle of Moet champagne in an ice filled bucket.

He stood, waiting for payment. Sebastian hesitated, eyeing the female on the dance floor, until, pausing for a rest, she made her way to the opposite end of the bar. Then, when she was in direct view of where he stood, Sebastian pulled out a thick wad of one hundred dollar bills with deliberate ease.

"You're scopin' hard," Robert remarked, sliding over to him.

"Is it that obvious?"

Robert smiled as he called the bartender over to him, pointing to the Moet bottle, and then holding up two fingers. "If you want to get someone's attention," he explained, "you got to do it in style."

The bartender brought out two more gleaming buckets filled with ice and champagne and placed them in front of Robert and Sebastian. Soon, Nick joined them at the bar.

"We plannin' a party?" Nick quipped.

"It seems Sebastian is," explained Robert, nodding in the direction of the females at the far edge. "I'm in for the ride—you?" Nick nodded, and Robert leaned over and gave instructions to the bartender, who then pulled out three more glasses and headed across the bar.

"Ladies, the gentlemen at the other end of the bar sent these over," the bartender explained, setting up three long stemmed champagne glasses in front of the red haired woman and her friends.

Smiling, she leaned in to confer with her crew. She then took up one of the glasses and held it up momentarily in recognition of their newfound admirers.

"Let's go, boys," Robert declared, grabbing the champagne bottle as he headed towards the females.

It was clear which woman belonged to whom. Sebastian staked out his claim from the outset.

The throbbing music made conversation difficult, yet their bodies came closer, moving in unison to the rhythm.

It was two hours later that Sebastian walked out of Geo holding her arm.

"I'm okay. You don't have to hold me up," she said, shrugging his hand away.

"You sure about that?" he inquired, pulling out a ten dollar bill to tip the valet.

"Yeah...I can handle it...nice car."

"Thanks."

"3.2 liter V6...Audi makes a pretty efficient engine," she remarked. Sebastian stared at her in surprise.

"I studied engineering in school," she replied, folding a wisp of hair behind her ear. "...runs in the family."

Sebastian nodded as he turned the ignition over, bringing the car to life. "You're just full of interesting info, aren't you?"

She smiled coyly.

He turned to check her out. The short hemline of her red dress, pulled up by the slant of the seat, revealed the pink flesh of her inner thigh.

All this is mine, he thought as he sped off.

In the morning he heard her getting dressed. She waited at the foot of the bed looking at him for any sign of acknowledgment to justify their night together. But, not wanting, not able to look at her, he feigned sleep rather than talk.

It was too much of a hassle exchanging words, telling them you'll call them, and that you had a great time. Why can't they just leave?

He fell back asleep. The door slammed shut. Two hours later, he was more sluggish than usual. A shower should do the trick, he

17

thought. He stepped out of the shower and decided to stay home that day. He sank into the sofa and clicked on the Knicks game. Finally, it seemed they were going to win.

A few hours later the phone rang. He let it ring. The machine picked up; the dial tone was all that remained of the caller. Slowly, Sebastian stood up. His body ached. On the television, a pitchman extolled the benefits of SUPRACLEAN, the most effective multi-purpose cleaner in the world!

The clock on the wall read 4:30. Sleep had overpowered him. He rubbed his head, unsure of where the day went. The phone rang again. Annoyed at the prospect of talking to anyone just then, he decided to let the machine pick it up once more. The dial tone was all that remained. Again the phone rang. This time Sebastian felt he needed to get it.

HELLO!

"Sebastian?"

"Who's this?"

"Isabella...from last night."

"Oh. Hi. ...How'd you get my number?"

"You gave it to me. Don't you remember?

"Yeah. Sure I do," Sebastian replied, his voice consciously softer. "So, what's going on?"

"Not much. How about you?"

"Same old."

"I had a good time last night."

"Yeah, I had a ball," replied Sebastian, quickly looking at the wall clock again

"I was really drunk," Isabella said with a nervous laugh

"Yeah, I know. So was I." An uncomfortable silence filled up the empty space between them.

"You still there?" he asked

"Yes, I'm here."

"Listen, I gotta go. Maybe we can talk later."

"Yeah. Sure"

"O.K ....bye."

"Bye." He held up the phone to his ear. A few moments later, the ring tone let him know there was no one there.

Sebastian's head was splitting now. He trudged into the bathroom and opened the medicine cabinet, rapidly swallowing a couple of aspirins with some water. He leaned over the sink for a moment, hoping the aspirin would take care of the throbbing in his brain. He closed the cabinet door and tried to hold his head up. In the mirror, his reflection looked back at him. Quickly, Sebastian shut the lights.

Nothing is less in our power than the heart, and far from commanding we are forced to obey it.
Jean Jacques Rousseau

The Heavy Heart

On MacDougal St. in Greenwich Village it is said that life is accustomed to go on very few hours of sleep. So much happens on this particular street at any given hour, that rarely is there a lull in activity. For the student of the senses and the lover of life there is no other place in the world more suitable to live and thrive. But what does a person hungry for isolation, for lofty remoteness where people and things are muted into the background—what does he feel about this particular stretch of New York City real estate? To that person, living on what many say is one of the distinguished streets in American culture—where music and poetry was listened to and loved—living here is an unending source of hellish irritation.

James Nickels, then, was upset when he walked out of his apartment building onto MacDougal St. and found himself jostled by bustling humanity going about their day. "Too many freakin' people," he thought, maneuvering his way to the corner light to hail down a yellow taxicab. It stopped at the red light and he jumped in.

"Fifty-sixth and seventh," he barked through the open partition separating the front from the back. "I'm in a hurry, so try to make it quick."

"What is that, sir?" The driver replied, looking in the rear view mirror. "I am sorry, sir. I did not hear you."

James didn't reply immediately, but instead stared at the eyes looking back at him in the rearview mirror. "Fiiifffty ssssixth aaand ssseeventh," he drawled sarcastically. "Don't you speak English?"

"Sir, I am new in America. Five months here." The driver replied, a wide smile on his face. It seemed he was of Indian origin.

"Congratulations."

James looked out the window. The promise of rain hung heavy in the clouds. The light turned green; the cab accelerated and James glanced at the building he emerged from minutes earlier. A gust of wind suddenly blew a discarded Daily News onto the front steps. Javier, the doorman, rushed to pick it up.

"Filthy place," James thought. "I really need to get the hell out of here." The driver glanced once more into the rearview mirror and saw James rubbing his chest.

"You okay?"

"It's nothing." James debated for a split second and said, "Thanks."

For some time now, James Nickels, a man of thirty-eight, still ambitious to conquer the world, with plans of going very far in life, was worried about his health, particularly his heart. It began slightly: a dull ache when he woke in the morning; a sharp, brief pang after a meal, none of which worried him enough to give it serious thought. But as time went on the dull ache grew in intensity, and what was a fleeting pang and a passing thought became a continuous throb and a constant worry.

He had to do something about it—it couldn't go on this way! His business, so crucial to his plans for the future, was suffering

21

because of the time worrying about the "health situation." His mortality became an uninvited guest, one he didn't like hanging around.

The door to Dr. Samuel's office opened a little too easily for James. You hardly had to push it before it gave way entirely. Those hinges need to be changed, he thought as he sat down in the waiting room.

He picked up a copy of *Architectural Digest* to the right of him. A loud bang, indicating the entrance of another person, distressed the hush of the office. The secretary looked up and said to no one in particular, "We really have to fix that door."

James walked over to it. He studied it carefully for a few minutes, ultimately resting his gaze on the hinges that formed the spine of the door.

"The doctor must be real popular," he called out across the room. The secretary looked up, startled by the unexpected comment directed at her.

"Why do you say that?" she replied out of curiosity.

"Well, he must have lots of people walking through here; the hinges are worn thin." James thoughtfully ran his hand down the edge of the uppermost part of the door. "You need to replace them," he called out.

"Uh…thank you. I'll make sure to tell the doctor."

James handled the door, opening it and closing it in turns as if in a trance, unaware of the eyes staring at him. Then, emerging from the reverie, he shut it, looked around uncomfortably and returned to his seat.

Those people, perhaps, would not have thought his behavior so strange, had they known that doors were somewhat of a passion for James Nickels. In fact, his success in acquiring and selling profitable businesses depended on a simple secret: upon entering an establishment he took very careful notice of the front door. A good sign, one that meant profit, was if the door opened easily, indicating an impressive amount of humanity entering—and a moneymaking acquisition!

After formalities were disposed of, he would ask, to the bewilderment of the owner and everyone present, how many times the hinges on the front door were changed. If a satisfactory answer was given, James would go forward with the deal, assured he was on the right track.

There was that dilapidated Laundromat on 34th and 9th: good cash flow, minimal overhead—and he had been lead to it by a joke that the place was so run down the owner had to change doors every year.

The fools! While they joked, he found it was a central location used by tourists from four nearby hotels. He approached the tired owner, offered to take it off his hands as is, and a deal was struck.

But what did it mean, this loosely hinged door at a heart doctor's office? He fidgeted in his seat uncomfortably. A reproduction of Van Gogh's *Starry Night* on the wall across from him caught his attention momentarily. Then he reached over for a magazine on the stand to the lower right.

"Mr. Nickels."

James stood up and followed the nurse into the examination room. "Put this on, please," the nurse instructed, handing him a smock. James looked around the room. Pictures of glistening blue waters and soothing sunsets overlooked a neat, sterile space.

Ten minutes later, Dr. Samuels walked into the room, a wide smile on his face.

"How are you, Mr. Nickels?"

"Not so good, doc. ...can't get rid of these chest pains."

"Let's take a look," said Dr. Samuels as he withdrew the chart from the slot on the door and examined it. "I see your primary doctor ordered a complete evaluation." He flipped to the next page, scanned its contents and paused midway down.

"Why don't we get started so we can find out the problem," he declared. "It should take no more than two hours." Dr. Samuels placed the chart under his arm, smiled and said, " I'm sure we'll find out what it is."

"I hope so doc. I really can't go on like this." James pleaded. The doctor continued to smile reassuringly as he opened the door.

*   *   *

The information James received that afternoon weighed heavy on his mind as he entered the front door of his apartment. How could it happen to him?—An enlarged heart! *A matter of not enough blood getting to the heart... the heart works too hard,* the doctor said *...careful or you will put yourself in extreme danger.*

It was all too bewildering for him. His future had looked promising, and full of possibilities: money, influence, and a family with Sandra. The doctor had to be wrong. Wasn't he too young to be going through this? He hung up the brown leather jacket Sandra bought him last year. He paused, feeling the urge to check the hinges of the front door. He stepped towards it.

James twisted the doorknob and opened it. For some time he stood there, swinging the door back and forth, his thoughts in a whirlwind.

What had he done to deserve this? Damn it!—Was he being punished? Ten minutes went by before he stopped suddenly, startled by his loss of awareness. Closing the door one last time, he looked around and headed to the bedroom.

A dull sense of fear ran through James as he sat on the edge of the bed. It was late afternoon. Through the window, James watched as the sun perched itself high up in the sky, beckoning everyone to notice before her departure later that evening.

He sat there till the room darkened, as the light, streaming in through the windows, gave way to the shadows brought on by impending night. Suddenly, he arose, undressed and walked to the refrigerator to get a bottle of Heineken. He then staggered to the living room and turned on the television. What seemed like hours passed before he was aware Sandra, his wife, had arrived home.

"James, I've been calling you for five minutes. Haven't you heard me?"

"Huh….no…I mean, yeah…

"For God's sake, James," Sandra cried out." I needed your help with the groceries. They were too heavy for me. Didn't you hear me? I must've called your name ten times."

James turned up the volume, drowning Sandra's voice in a sea of sound blaring from the television.

"James, are you listening to me or am I talking to myself once again?"

"I'm sorry, honey; I'm really into this movie." Once more, he turned up the volume.

Sandra sat down at the kitchen table for a few minutes, trying to bring composure to her agitated mind. She wanted to be kind now, to understand James now. He often shut her out—that wasn't something new, but tonight she wasn't going to erupt; she had done too much of that already. Tonight was going to be different. The news from the doctor couldn't be good, she thought. They were going to have dinner and talk about it, he said on the phone. She chopped the tomatoes carefully. Bolognese sauce: that was his favorite.

The smells from the kitchen wafted out to the living room. James became aware of the aroma and said so.

Sandra stuck her head out. "Spaghetti Bolognese. It'll be ready in a little while."

He turned back to the television. A dark hue had enveloped the room. He sat up again, suddenly aware of the darkness. It frightened him. Quickly, he walked over to the light switch and flipped it on.

From his vantage point he could see into the kitchen where Sandra was preparing dinner. Her shape, her long brownish hair, stirred him and he approached her.

He placed his hands on her waist, nuzzling his face into her neck. Sandra jumped, startled by his unexpected touch. He shifted suggestively, moving his hands up and down her waist.

"James...I'm cooking...not now," she said. His fingers were in her hair now, brushing it aside so he could kiss the back of her neck. He pressed himself closer.

"James...please...I said not now."

"C'mon, you know it's been awhile," he replied hoarsely.

"Yeah, but now isn't the time. I have to cook."

He pushed away from her forcefully. She flinched, her husband's gesture striking her like an imaginary body blow.

"Fine! Let him get his own goddamn dinner!" she thought, turning the stove off, and storming into the bedroom. The Bolognese sauce bubbled mischievously for some time before, its energy exhausted, it flattened, half cooked, with no one to encourage it further.

It was late into the evening before Sandra ventured into the living room again. James slumped on the couch. Flickering light emanated from the television as his head perched awkwardly on his left shoulder.

"James." He didn't answer.

"James!"

She stood in the same position for a minute more before retreating into the kitchen. He's doing it on purpose, she thought as she sat there furiously turning the pages of the day's newspaper. The silence coming from the living room threatened to overwhelm her. She resolved to talk to him.

"James," she called out to the other room, "James, ...you hear me... I want to talk." He didn't answer. Sandra tossed the newspaper and walked into the living room. It was dark save for the faint light the TV threw out. She could hardly see his face.

"James, wake up, I need to talk to you." She nudged him gently.

" James, c'mon, wake up please." She pushed him with greater force.

"James…James?…James! Oh my God!!

There is still, however, a third partner to the relation of Edith and Jim. That partner is the world as a whole. ... Too often, however, two people come together in the marriage bond, or otherwise, and use their high estimate of each other to depreciate, and even hate, the world in general. (p.171)

Eli Siegel
From *SELF AND WORLD: An Explanation of Aesthetic Realism*

Comfort

When Michael Hardsworth and Samantha Peterson married on a bright June afternoon when the peonies were in full bloom, they had high hopes for one another and for the future. On that day amidst many congratulations, an abundance of well-catered food and smiles that seemed to go on forever, every so often, when it seemed they could talk, Michael and Samantha would turn to each other as if to say something. But, alas, conversation between the two was not to be that day.

That night as they lay in each other's arms, body rapturously touching body, and spoke about possibilities to come, the words that needed to be said—to be said desperately—seemed less important.

Two years after that day of sacred vows and life long promises, we find Michael and Samantha Hardsworth sitting together for a dinner of beef tenderloins, in a fashionable apartment in Greenwich Village, NY, overlooking Washington Square Park.

Outside, the moon is full and a wonder to behold, its rays casting a soft glow on objects and people. Yet, it is unseen by our couple, who prefer instead to close the shades that evening, sacrificing luminosity for dim ambience.

The light is turned down while two lone candlesticks on the table bathe the apartment in a soft hue, creating a dance of shadows on the walls and ceiling. A song can be heard playing in the background.

You are my laaaadyyyyy, you are my love...

"I don't know why she said that to me. I really didn't do anything to her," said Samantha, cutting a tender piece of beef.

You're everything I neeeeeed, yeah, yeah.

"Why do you even waste your time talking about her? You know Harriet is just mad that you're married and she's not. She's been like that since you first met her," replied Michael.

You are my lady, you are–

Good evening ladies and gentlemen. We interrupt our regular broadcast to bring you this important news.

"I don't know why though. Ever since I began working at the office, I never did anything to her but want to be friends with her."

The first air strikes have been launched against Slovakia by a narrow coalition of American and British forces.

"You have to be careful. Most people—wait a second.

Word from the pentagon indicates that the strikes will not be directed towards civilians, but rather at Slovakia's existing sanitation and electrical systems.

"Did you hear that, honey? They've begun bombing," said Michael through a mouthful of beef.

The James administration has gone forward even as polls show that almost 50% of Americans are against military action.

"Its about time! I was so tired of them just talking and talking about it," hissed Samantha, upset at the interruption.

"Yeah, it is about time they go after that dictator!" declared Michael, spearing an asparagus tip.

Officials say the strikes are designed to produce minimal collateral damage.

"Oh, shut it off. It's depressing me," said Samantha " Sweetie, I thought we were going to have a nice romantic dinner together."

"We are. I just want to hear the end of this."

Critics say the Slovakian people are already devastated from a decade of U.S. led economic sanctions that have left 500,000 children dead from disease, and that a military strike would plunge the country into a humanitarian crises never before seen in hist--. (click)

"I hope it's a quick war. I sure don't want too many soldiers to die," Michael mused, as he turned the radio off. He looked at Samantha's disinterested face and thought it would be better to change the subject quickly. "Like I was saying, people don't like it when something good happens to you. I learned early on that you only have your family and maybe one or two close friends in life. That's it."

Samantha looked at her husband, agitated by something she couldn't put her finger on. It's that damn Harriet, she thought, as if trying to convince herself of something. "You know, you're right. My problem is I'm too trusting of people."

"You're only going to get hurt in the long run," Michael replied soothingly, as he sliced the last piece of tenderloin on his plate. He smiled at his wife and meditated on whether they should have this dish more than once a week.

31

"I guess that's how people are," Samantha half-heartedly declared with a sigh.

"Are you going to eat those?" Michael asked, pointing his knife towards the barely touched meat on Samantha's plate.

"No...be my guest," she replied, shoving her plate across the table.

She stared at him for a moment. Stuffing his face—that's all he thinks about. Her eyes bore down on her husband. Outside a car horn blared, and a dog barked three times.

"These are so good. I could eat like this every night," Michael exclaimed, greedily pouring the contents of his wife's remaining dinner onto his plate.

He's definitely eating too much these days, she thought, twirling a lock of hair around her finger.

Her eyes wandered to his nose, which for the first time seemed to bulge out disproportionately. It had always been a bit big, but how big she hadn't noticed before.

It was as if Michael was undergoing a slight but ever so real metamorphosis right in front of her very eyes. She continued to look at him and wondered why she hadn't noticed these imperfections before. She sipped from her merlot, her eyes surveying her spouse of two years. Michael flashed Samantha a toothy grin in between chews, and then proceeded to hum contentedly.

"I really wish you wouldn't do that," she exclaimed.

"What?

"You know...hum while you're eating. It's disgusting."

"I always do that," he stated, a hint of hurt in his voice.

"That doesn't make it right," she replied. 'It's bad manners."

"Bad manners…yeah right."

They sat in silence for some time, until, like the suddenness of glass shattering, she joked, "Be careful, Michael. You don't want to get fat."

"Don't worry about me, *honey*. You know I have the metabolism of a horse." He beat his chest one time.

She stood and headed for the kitchen. He followed her with his eyes until her shape disappeared from view.

It became quiet. He was getting used to the silence between them.

When they first met it seemed there wasn't enough time in the day for all the things they wanted to tell each other. This ease of conversation, the feeling he could explore the universe through and with another person, was the chief reason Michael asked Samantha for her hand in marriage. But as time went on conversations dwindled down to the point where silences, long and deafening, became the norm. It dawned on Michael that they were reaching a point where they had nothing to say to each other.

One day terror overtook him as he watched an old rerun of a sitcom he once liked, alone in their spacious living room. Was this all of it? Were they to spend the rest of their lives this way? He ran to the shower and tried to drown his doubts in a warm cascade of water.

But soon, the fright seemed to subside amidst the routine of life, and Michael changed his mind about the silences that occurred more frequently between the two of them. He began to feel it was sometimes easier not to talk.

"They aren't so bad," he thought to himself as he inserted the plates into the dishwasher, later that evening. "Every now and then silences can be healthy between husband and wife."

The sound of rushing water signaled Samantha's intention to take her nightly bath. He finished drying off the dishes, packed away the last remnants of tenderloin into the fridge and headed to the couch to read that day's Daily News. Within minutes he was fast asleep, the newspaper draped over his chest.

"Michael, wake up," Samantha said, shaking him gently as she stood over him, her hair wet and curly. "Michael…Michael, wake up. I want to tell you something."

"What is it, Samantha? Can't you see I'm sleeping?" Michael turned over to his side, his back to her.

Samantha shook him with greater vehemence. "C'mon, Michael…will you please get up…I have to talk to you!"

"What is it for God's sake!" Michael shouted, sitting up suddenly.

Samantha winced, surprised at her husband's sharp response. She looked at him with a shocked expression.

"I'm sorry honey….I don't know what got over me. "I haven't gotten much sleep lately."

He searched Samantha's face for any sign of forgiveness.

"No! Forget about it. Go back to sleep," she blurted as she turned to walk away.

He grabbed her arm. "Oh, come on. How many times do I have to say it—sorry!" Samantha struggled half heartedly to rid herself of his touch. "Just sit down and talk to me. I promise I'll listen." She sat down on the couch beside Michael, her features softening a bit.

"It's Harriett…the whole situation is bothering me." She turned to him and said, "You know, maybe it's my fault she's angry."

"How could it be your fault? What have you done to her?"

"Well, I always talk about us…what we're doing. I never ask what's happening in her life, what she's worried about."

"So, what's wrong with that? If she wanted to talk about herself she would say something. She probably thinks your life is more interesting, that's all."

"But don't you see? That's what I've been saying to myself all this time—that my life *is* more interesting than hers. That's the problem." Samantha looked at Michael intently, as if she was waiting for him to respond with an answer that would ease her growing agitation.

But he did not know what to say.

"Oh, come on," he replied finally. "What are you getting so worked up about? You're making a big deal out of nothing. You'll see that everything's okay when you go into the office tomorrow. Harriett will be fine and you'll see you were all wrong." He reached for the remote control on the coffee table directly in front of him, signaling the end of the conversation. She lingered a few seconds more on the couch next to him before departing silently to the bedroom. Michael clicked on the newly installed sixty inch flat screen television.

For the next half-hour he surfed through the channels, searching for something to watch but not really looking at anything. At about midnight he gave up, clicked the television off and headed for bed, weary and agitated.

The next day, on his way home from work, he was troubled by the previous night's conversation with Samantha. He bought a bouquet of lilies, her favorite flower. He headed home early, hoping to surprise her.

"Samantha."

"Samantha, I'm home."

"Samantha, honey, I'm home. Where are you?"

Michael stood there for some time, waiting for a reply. But none came.

The Gift

She was a mystery to him, more so now than ever before. Sitting there like she had done countless other times since they were married, Sybil seemed changed to Jeffrey Drummond in a way that stirred him, made him feel both wonder and fear. For you see, the couple had just returned from the doctor who told them, in unequivocal terms, that Sybil was pregnant.

"Jeffrey, are you O.K?" asked Sybil, catching him looking intently at her.

"Uh...yeah," he replied, feeling a bit awkward for staring. He walked over to their black leather couch and sat down beside her. Turning with a smile, he said, "I can't believe we're going to be parents in eight months. It's amazing."

"Yes...it is," she said, momentarily meeting his glance before returning to the magazine she was reading.

The ticking from the ornate grandfather clock across from them filled the silence between them.

"Are you happy?" he suddenly asked.

"Yes...I'm happy," Sybil said, trying to smile. "...a little worried about whether my health will hold up. I'm just scared, that's all." She held the gaze of her husband for a few more minutes before turning to the magazine once again.

'Let's try and be happy," he replied, reaching for her hand.

"I said I was." Sybil drew back her arm.

Jeffrey didn't know what to say. He lingered for a few minutes by the couch, waiting for Sybil to say more. When she didn't, he walked over to the bookshelf, pretending to look intently for something that wasn't there, hoping that she would, eventually, say something. When it seemed nothing else was forthcoming, he went into the kitchen, poured himself another cup of the Colombian coffee she had brewed earlier, and sat down at the breakfast bar.

When Jeffrey Drummond and Sybil Reston first married they affirmed to one another that having a child was in their future. In the years since, there were more conversations on the subject, and it seemed as the months went along that the hope to become parents would turn into a living, breathing reality. They had known for a few weeks there was a real possibility that Sybil was pregnant, what with the home pregnancy test coming back positive.

Yet Jeffrey was confused. He thought women were supposed to be ecstatic at being pregnant. Where were the tears, the long glances into one another's eyes as plans for the future of the unborn child were discussed with frequent kisses interrupting?

He thought a lot that night, staying up even after his wife went to bed. The clock read a quarter to eleven. The rumbling in his stomach led him to the GE Frigidaire they recently purchased. Rummaging through the packed shelves for a minute, he suddenly slammed it shut.

"Nothing to eat," he grumbled.

"Jeff, is everything all right?" Sybil called out from the bedroom.

"Yeah, "he exclaimed. "Just hungry."

"I went shopping this afternoon. You have roast beef in the bottom fridge drawer."

He stood in their newly renovated kitchen, examining the French ceramic tiles with his toes. A crack in the grout made him bend down on one knee to take a closer look. "Damn contractor," he mumbled.

Ten minutes later he took his usual walk around the house, making sure everything was locked and the alarm system was turned on. At the front door he decided to step outside quickly, hoping the cool autumn night would refresh him and, perhaps, clear his thoughts.

It was an hour before midnight now. A chilly breeze in the air rustled the fallen leaves, carrying them from place to place like wandering, tired travelers. Jeffrey breathed in deeply and then went back inside. A half-hour later he was fast asleep.

The next morning, promptly at six a.m., Jeffrey woke up and went through his usual morning routine: he dressed, wolfed down some eggs and whole wheat toast and was about to run out the door when suddenly he felt something was amiss. He went back inside, walked up to the bedroom and looked at Sybil sound asleep.

Standing in the doorway, he was struck by the miracle that was going to take place in the upcoming months; one that had occurred an unimaginable number of times in the history of the world, but which, for Jeffrey, seemed to be happening for the first time in the body of a woman who seemed so much a stranger.

The dark outside was giving way to dawn now, and the sounds of beginning day could be faintly heard in the distance. He leaned over the bed and kissed his wife on the forehead before leaving for work.

Reliant Real Estate was buzzing with the activity of Monday morning preparations for the coming week. Jeffrey walked straight to his desk and past Sam Weitz, his co-worker. Preoccupied with thoughts of his wife and the coming birth, he didn't hear the loud "GOOD MORNING!" Sam yelled from the office next door. Another loud greeting and Jeffrey was startled out of himself.

"Tone it down over there, Sam. It's Monday, for God's sake."

"If you had heard me the first time, I wouldn't have had to yell. You going' deaf?" cried Sam.

"No, not deaf…just a little crazy."

"What's that?"

"Nothing…sorry… lots on my mind," replied Jeffrey, looking around for a pen with which to write. Hearing the change in Jeffrey's voice, Sam walked over to see what was wrong.

"You all right, buddy?" he asked, making himself comfortable on the three man couch in the far corner of Jeffrey's office.

"Yeah, I'm okay," Jeffrey replied, looking up and forcing a smile. "…In fact, I'm great. Sybil and I just found out we're going to have a baby."

"Heyyy! Congratulations, big guy!" exclaimed Sam, a grin on his face. "I knew it was bound to happen soon," he said, throwing his legs up on the coffee table.

"Where the hell did I put all my pens?" Jeffrey exclaimed, searching his desk in frustration.

"Relax buddy, you can have mine," Sam said, chucking a silver Bick across the room. "Sooo! Big time for you and Sybil."

"Yeah… it is," replied Jeffrey, concentrating on the paper work in front of him.

Sam began to whistle. Jeffrey continued with the work in front of him. A tapping sound soon took the place of the whistle. A few more minutes passed and Sam began to believe his co-worker did not want to talk. He thought, perhaps, a change of surroundings would encourage Jeffrey to say more.

"Hey, how about lunch today at that new Italian place, Villa Roma…you know, to celebrate?" Sam asked, jumping up from the couch.

Jeffrey hesitated. "I don't know. I got a lot on my mind."

"That's exactly why you should come out for lunch with me. We need to talk. You don't look so good."

He had a faint notion Sam was right; he would feel better talking to someone. He glanced at his co-worker. Sam stuck his pinky finger in his ear and rubbed vigorously

"I don't know. I really should head home."

"C'mon, an hour won't kill you, " replied Sam.

"All right…O.K. Maybe you're right," Jeffrey mumbled.

"Good. Lunch is on me," exclaimed Sam as he walked out the door. "See you at 12:30."

By the time Jeffrey met Sam for lunch, thoughts of Sybil kept insisting themselves. Why did she seem sad? They had planned everything: where to live, the number of years she was going to stay with the baby, even the color of the room. What was going on with her? Why the hell wasn't she happy? These questions knocked about in Jeffrey's head as he walked into the restaurant, glad for the diversion which lunch with Sam would hopefully provide.

Villa Roma was filled with tables so crowded together conversations became part of the public domain, and the term rubbing elbows frequently took on a literal meaning. Waiters with Italian accents darted between their tables and the kitchen, yelling at busboys to clean up in preparation for the next patron. Aromas emanating from all sorts of heaping dishes inflamed appetites and made mouths yearn. It was one of those places, unpretentious and charming, where the food was delicious, and that was all that mattered.

They ordered before either broached a conversation. Finally, as he grabbed a piece of bread from the basket, Sam said, "Jeff, I don't understand something. If you're so happy, why'd you walk in this morning like someone died?"

"I'm happy—what are you talking about?"

"C'mon, how long have we worked together?"

"Sam, I've only been in the job for two months," replied Jeffrey, a quizzical expression on his face.

Sam chomped on a piece of bread. "Two months, two years— what's the difference? I feel like I've known you forever."

Jeffrey gazed at Sam grinning between mouthfuls of buttered bread. If he didn't talk to someone he would burst. Sam would have to do. "I should be happy...I am happy...I think...but I feel like Sybil isn't. I don't understand why. I mean, isn't having a baby what a woman wants?"

"I know exactly what you mean. When Samantha was pregnant it was a real surprise to see her upset sometimes. After all the conversations we had about having children, I thought she'd be jumping up for joy." Jeffrey listened carefully.

"So what did you do?" he asked.

"What could I do?" answered Sam nonchalantly; "I put on a smile and gave her lots of hugs and kisses for nine months."

"That's it?"

"There was nothing the matter with her. That's how pregnant women are. You'll get to know that soon enough. By the second child you'll be a pro at it. Look at me: when my youngest was born I was watching a football game outside in the waiting room.

"You gotta be kidding me?"

"I'm telling you the truth," replied Sam, buttering another piece of bread. He looked at Jeffrey's surprised expression and let out a little chuckle. "Listen, I know right now you want to read books and find out as much as you can about having a baby, but don't worry, that will pass. Ultimately," he leaned into the conversation, pointing upwards with a butter-smeared knife, "what happens is in the hands of the big guy upstairs."

Sam leaned back and smiled at Jeffrey, who sat there in disbelief. Was he really thinking too much? Should he just chalk it up to feminine biology? How appealing!

Their meal arrived, and the two men began to eat. Neither one resumed the subject, preferring, it seemed, to talk about office politics for the rest of the time.

"Listen," Sam said as they walked out of the restaurant an hour later. "Why don't you and Sybil come over for dinner Friday night? It'll give a chance for the wives to talk."

Jeffrey thought about it for a few seconds before replying, "I don't know how Sybil will feel about it."

"Oh, she'll love to come," answered Sam. "It's been years since she saw Samantha."

"They've never met."

"My point exactly."

"Uhm...I'm not sure. "

"C'mon, it'll be fun."

"Well...all right."

"Great. Say about eight o'clock."

After work that day, Jeffrey decided to take the longer way home, hoping to see the brilliant orange and reds of the fall foliage. There was something about autumn that made him hopeful, the way nature seemed breathtakingly alive even as it gave way to winter.

"Sybil!" Jeffrey called out as he stepped into the foyer and hung his jacket in the crowded coat closet. They didn't live like kings, but they were comfortable enough, he often thought.

"I'm in the living room," she called back.

"Hey, how are you?" he asked, bending down to plant a kiss on her cheek.

"Nauseous, but doing okay," she replied, flipping through a magazine. "I was just reading these articles about the types of vitamins pregnant women should take."

"Yeah, you have to take care of yourself now," Jeffrey quipped. "There are two of you to think about."

An annoyed look flashed across Sybil's face.

"Everything okay?" Jeffrey asked, suddenly aware that something he said had upset her.

"Everything's fine. I'm just a little nauseous. That's all."

"You remember Sam from the office?"

"I think so," Sybil replied. "Doesn't he have a wife named Samantha?"

"Yeah, that's him. Well, he invited us for dinner Friday night and I told him we would come."

"I wish you would ask me before you accept invitations from people," she grumbled.

"What's the big deal?" he replied, disturbed by his wife's irritation. "It's only dinner. Besides it'll give you a chance to talk to Samantha. She's been pregnant a few times."

"You don't have to walk around feeling nauseous all the time. That's the big deal! What if I'm sitting at dinner and I can't stand the smell of the food. What do I do then?

"Listen, why don't we call Samantha and ask her what the best thing to do is."

"That's not the point!" Sybil cried, slapping the magazine shut. Husband and wife stared at each other for a long minute. Finally, she sighed and said, "We can go. It's no big deal. I just wish you asked me before you said yes, that's all." She clicked the television on. Jeffrey lumbered into the kitchen.

It wasn't how he expected her to react. Sitting there in the kitchen, Sam's words came back to him. So soothing in their triteness, they called out *That's how pregnant women are. You'll get used to it.*

The rich aroma of the coffee brewing wafted through the air, pleasantly distracting Jeffrey from the thoughts going on in his mind. He poured himself a cup, and pulled up a chair.

That Friday evening as they arrived at the house, Sam greeted them at the door with a big smile. "It's been a long time since the two of you have been here," he said jovially.

"Sam, we've never been here. I told you that already," Jeffrey remarked.

"Like I said, it's been a long time." He smiled at Sybil and pointed at Jeffrey. "This one's a real stickler for details. Sheesh!"

He ushered them into the spacious living room. Pearl white porcelain tiles reflected the light beaming from the ornate crystal chandelier suspended above their heads. Across from where they stood, a growing fire flickered playfully within the marble encased fireplace. Above a sixty inch television hung proudly.

"Your home is lovely," Sybil remarked.

"Thank you," replied Sam, beaming contentedly. "We just finished doing the kitchen. Let me show you around." We recently got a new living room set. Come, I'll show it to you." They walked into the living room together, Sam pointing to all his recent purchases with pride as if they were trophies on exhibition.

"SAMANTHAAAAA," yelled Sam into the kitchen, "JEFFREY AND SYBIL ARE HERE! Samantha Weiss walked out a minute later.

A heavy set woman in her early thirties, she walked with the determination of someone used to having her way. Her thin, black hair was pulled tightly into a bun that sat neatly on the back of her head. A thickly encrusted diamond ring seemed to weigh heavily on

46

her fourth finger. "Hello! Good to meet you," she exclaimed, extending a hand out to Sybil. "So good to see you."

"How come it's taken you all this time to come over?" asked Samantha as she led Sybil into the dining room with Jeffrey and Sam following. "I've told Sam a million times to invite the two of you for dinner." She turned to Sybil and said quietly, "He probably forgot. It's just like him." Samantha giggled. Sybil suddenly noticed the painting behind her. "Well, it doesn't matter, you're here now and I'm glad."

"Me too," replied Sybil, quickly attentive to her hostess. "It'll give us a chance to get to know each other."

The meal was a real treat for Jeffrey. He couldn't help admiring the array of the dishes laid out in front of him: Caesar Salad, Roast Turkey, Halibut, and a Chocolate Mouse he could not stop eating.

"You're a lucky man, Sam, to have a wife that cooks as well as Samantha does," declared Jeffrey as the dishes were cleared from the table.

"Oh, this is nothing. She did a little extra tonight because we knew you were coming, but this is pretty regular stuff." Sam wiped his lips and sat back heavily.

"Still though," Jeffrey replied, "I know if I had to cook every night it would tire me out."

"You gotta be kidding me, right?" Sam said incredulously. He let out a slight chuckle and threw a glance towards the kitchen. "What else does she have to do?"

Jeffrey sat up in surprise.

He was aware of thoughts like these in himself. In fact, there were times when he believed strongly in them. But that someone had the temerity to actually say them aloud came as a shock.

"C'mon," declared Sam breaking the silence, "you don't really think I say these things to her." He chortled again. "Are you for real? She would kill me. Let's just say its what I expect and she gets the message. It works out fine like that." Sam picked up his glass of wine and finished off its contents with one swig. He looked intently at Jeffrey as he picked up the delicately embroidered napkin on his right and wiped his mouth slowly.

"You mean to tell me you never felt the same way, Jeff? You're a liar if you say no." Jeffrey glanced at Sybil in the kitchen drying a plate Samantha handed to her.

"No, I have Sam. That's the scary part."

"Scary…what are you talking about? Why should you be scared? That's how things are." Sam's voice was rising. Samantha and Sybil looked over at them momentarily. Sam, conscious of this, lowered his voice. "Samantha's happy, I'm happy—we're doing fine."

"How can you tell?" Jeffrey asked.

With a sudden awkward movement, Sam swiped the bottle of red wine with his arm, toppling it to the floor. It crashed loudly. On the floor, a blood red liquid covered the porcelain tiles.

"Damn it!" he cried in frustration, trying to avoid the growing puddle of wine.

'It's okay—no big deal—don't worry about it," called Samantha as she took out a mop and some paper towels from the kitchen cupboard. She handed two sheets to Sybil, who in turn handed one to Jeffrey in full expectation of his aid in the cleanup.

Ten minutes later, Sybil and Samantha were preparing dessert and Sam, a stony expression on his face, was back at the table with a fresh bottle of red wine.

So what were we talking about?" asked Jeffrey in an attempt at amiability.

"What is there to talk about?—I know how she feels, " grumbled Sam, focusing instead on using a corkscrew to open up the bottle. Jeffrey decided not to say anymore presently.

Grimacing, Sam inserted the corkscrew very carefully, making sure it was in the direct center so as to give the lever the greatest momentum when pulling it out, a feat he easily accomplished at the beginning of dinner but, which now seemed to be of the greatest difficulty; for every time success was at hand the corkscrew would diverge into another direction causing the cork, and in Jeffrey's opinion, its holder, to come apart.

"Damn it!" Sam exclaimed. "I just did it. I don't know what the hell the problem is?!"

"Maybe your nerves are a little frayed? Happens to me when something breaks. It's okay. I think I've had enough wine for the night. "

"I'm not nervous," Sam declared," his voice rising. "This is just a difficult bottle."

Sam continued wrestling with the bottle for five more minutes. Finally, he put the bottle aside with a look of disgust on his face. "Goddamn it!" he muttered.

"Don't worry about it," said Jeffrey, "like I said, I don't want any more wine. Was it an expensive bottle?"

"What is it with all these questions?" Sam replied heatedly. "You know what your problem is, Jeff? You can't let things be. You always have to ask questions about everything."

Just then Samantha arrived at the table with a tray laden with various desserts and fresh coffee. An hour later, Jeffrey and Sybil were on their way home.

"Did you have a good time?" Jeffrey asked as they drove through the moonlit road.

"Yeah," Sybil replied half-heartedly. She gazed out the window.

It was almost midnight now. Suddenly, Sybil turned the window down flooding the car with a rush of cool air.

"What are you doing? It's cold outside?" exclaimed Jeffrey, startled by the sudden wind.

"What a gorgeous night!" Sybil exclaimed, looking up at the heavens. A minute later, she turned the window up as they drove down the dark highway.

"Jeff?"

"Yeah?"

"Do you think our life will change drastically when the baby is born?" Sybil placed her right hand over the slight bulge of her stomach.

"No, not real—" Jeffrey came to a stop at a red light. To the right, blinking yellow lights notified drivers of the oncoming train. He paused for a moment, and then, turned to look at his wife. Their eyes met, and he said, "Yes, Samantha. I think it'll change a great deal."

She smiled.

Interlude

Sam Westerfield leaned back on the padded headrest. Jeremiah paused, allowing his friend time for what seemed to be needed contemplation. He searched his face for some idea of the thoughts within.

"You sure can tell em'." Sam finally said. His voice was livelier.

"Well thank you, sir. Learned that specific talent from my darlin' Bessie. May she rest in peace," Jeremiah replied.

"Bessie...that your wife?"

"Yes sir. The best a man this side of the Atlantic could hope for." Sam pushed himself up in the wheelchair with some difficulty, wincing along with the movements. Jeremiah leaned in to help.

"Know what you mean," said Sam hoarsely. My Angie was everything to me. When she left, it didn't seem like there was anything left to live for."

"Well, now, I'm not sure you're right about that," stated Jeremiah.

"Whatch you mean?" declared Sam, focusing a menacing look on his contrary friend. "Don't you think I know myself?"

Jeremiah smiled, looked up in the heavens for a moment before saying, "Well, to tell you the truth, I ain't too sure you do."

"Humph! Well now—ain't that a kick in the pants!" exclaimed Sam. More surprised than angry, he said, "Why don't you go on and tell me some more of them stories. They's sure as hell better than your dang philosophizing." Sam turned to face the sun.

"You sure now?" Jeremiah inquired, a mischievous grin on his face.

"Go on—I don't got all day. You know I *am* ninety."

"Yup, that's what they tell me."

"Well, you gonna tell me a story or what?"

A Golden Cage

The bell indicating the end of Mr. Cipher's eighth pd. English class rang punctually at 2:05 every day. David Cipher shut the book he was reading to the bustling eleven year olds in front of him and said, "We'll continue tomorrow." Suddenly, the sound of excited voices filled the room.

"See you manyana, Mr. Cipher," cried an Asian boy darting to the exit.

"All right, Huang. Don't forget about homework."

"I got it. See ya!"

"Bye, Mr. C," said a dark skinned girl with a bright smile.

"Goodbye, Jasmine. You read well today."

"Thank you," she replied, beaming.

As the last of his students piled out of the class, the tall, brown haired teacher returned to his desk to pack up. He noticed Benjamin Nussbaum still sitting at his desk, a book in hand.

"Ben, the dismissal bell rang."

"I know, Mr. Cipher. Gimme just five more minutes. These Greek gods are awesome." David smiled and gazed at the small figure in the back of the room, his head buried in the large book.

"You know what? Why don't you borrow it and return it when you're done." Immediately, a head popped up above the edge of *Illustrated Greek Myths* by Momentous Mason III.

"No way! Really?—That's so cool. I promise I'll take care of it!

"I trust you."

Benjamin closed the book carefully, placed it inside his book bag and slowly approached his teacher.

"That Cerberus dude, you know, the three headed dog...that's pretty wild."

"Yes it is," replied David.

"Can I ask you a question, Mr. Cipher?"

"Anything, Ben."

"Is there really such a place as Hades? You know the way the Greeks described it. Do dead people really go there? And if not, where do they go?" David meditated on the question for a few moments, deciding on what the proper answer should be. He began to formulate a response, but at the last minute decided against it.

"Where do they go, indeed!" He smiled at his inquisitive student." I don't really know, Benjamin. I think, though, if you keep reading, you might find out." Benjamin Nussbaum looked up thoughtfully at his teacher.

"You promise?"

David Cipher smiled and nodded. Benjamin tugged on his book bag and headed out the door.

"Ben." The young student stopped inches away from the front door.

"I'm really proud of you. You've come a long way this year." Ben flashed a big grin and said, "Thank you, Mr. Cipher. I can't wait to tell my dad! I'm going to be seeing him in a few days. See you tomorrow." David smiled, packed up his attaché case and headed home.

"Susan!" He called out from the foyer as he entered the apartment.

"In the kitchen."

"Hi there." She smiled at him warmly. He pecked her on the cheek and stole a slice of red pepper from the salad she was preparing for dinner.

"How was your day?" She asked, good naturedly smacking his hand away.

"You know, O.K."

"Yeah, tell me about it."

"You know the boy I've been talking about all year?"

"Benjamin?"

"Yeah, Benjamin Nussbaum. The one who's mom remarried—dad wasn't really around; the one who's had trouble reading." He reached over for a piece of cucumber. "Well, there was a breakthrough today. We've been reading Greek myths in class and he enjoyed them so much he took the book home." David paused, trying to recollect a thought. "By the way, we need to talk about the type of car we're going to buy. Should we get it fully loaded or not?"

Susan turned to face her husband. "Wait a second—I'm getting a little dizzy with the way you just switched subjects." She looked at him, a low murmur coming from the television served as backdrop for the conversation. "Forget the car for now."

"All I'm saying is we need to talk about the deal we're looking for before it runs out," he replied, sauntering into the living room.

"Let's try to get our priorities straight," Susan called from the kitchen, amidst chopping sounds, sharp and hard. "Oh, before I forget—your uncle called. He wants you to come over for dinner Friday night."

"Any special reason?" David replied, sticking his head back into the kitchen.

"Something about your cousin visiting. Why don't you call him?"

"Yeah, uh…okay," he replied, entering the bedroom to change out of his work clothes.

David sat on the edge of the bed, turned on the lamp and reached over for the telephone. He picked it up, stopped in midair and returned it to the receiver. He loosened his tie. Once more he picked up the phone, pressed a few digits and lingered momentarily before slamming it back on its cradle.

"You call him yet?" asked Susan as she placed the dinner settings on the table twenty minutes later. David walked out of the bedroom, one hand through a t-shirt.

"Huh, oh…no, not yet. I'll do it after dinner." She gave him a searching glance on the way back to the kitchen.

"Don't look at me like that," he said, "I said I'd call him after dinner."

"You always say that when your uncle calls, and then you call him back a couple of days later when it's too late. Call him now and see what he wants. What's the worst thing that could happen?" David stared at her as if transmitting the answer telepathically.

"Just call him," she pleaded.

57

He fell into the sofa, turned the television on, and proceeded to ignore the advice of his wife. Susan heard the TV and marched into the living room.

"David, honey, what are you doing?" She asked, a syrupy sweetness in her voice. He increased the volume on the television. Susan stood for a few minutes more before she returned to the kitchen, calling out, " David, if you want to eat tonight, you better call your uncle." He meditated on his wife's ultimatum and weighed the possible outcomes. Having come to a conclusion rather swiftly, he lowered the volume, picked up the telephone and dialed his uncle's home number.

*   *   *

His uncle, Samuel Cipher, was a man of impressions, one who always donated generously to the synagogue. He had stature in the community, evident in the front row seats reserved for him during the high holy days when you were lucky if there was room to stand.

People noticed Sammy—the house he lived in, the cars he possessed, all symbols of wealth carefully cultivated over the years.

So it followed then that when his nephew, Saul Caspit, an investment banker, stopped over on a business trip, Sammy invited him for dinner, eager to make a lasting impression on his wealthy relative. Life in America had treated Sammy well, and he made sure everyone knew it.

Dutifully, he made the phone calls to the family, one of them being David. It couldn't be helped, thought Sammy as he hung up with Susan. David was his older brother's son and not to invite him would be to insult his older sibling. It wasn't that he didn't like David. On the contrary, Sammy thought him an intelligent young man with potential, if only he would get out of teaching and apply himself to another field. It was a noble profession and all of that, but no real money involved. Money was the real measure of success. Everyone knew that, except, perhaps, his hardheaded nephew.

Late that night David lay in bed wide-awake and troubled by his thoughts. "What's the matter?" asked Susan.

"Nothing....why do you think something's the matter?"

"Because you toss and turn and kick me when something's on your mind."

"I do not!"

"Yes, you do." She paused to give him a chance to gather his thoughts. "Are you going to tell me what's wrong?" David let a few minutes go by before turning to face his wife.

"I don't know about going over to my uncle's house for dinner. He—"

"—Is it the same old thing again?" interrupted Susan. " Sam knows better than to start talking to you about career choices. Your father made it clear to him."

"It's not that. The dinner's for my cousin. Never met him, but I hear he's a rich one. You should've heard Sammy go on about him— *Be on time David. We don't keep investment bankers from Barclays waiting.*"

"Your uncle has had wealthy people over for dinner before. Why the anxiety this time?"

"I don't know." David turned to lie on his back. " I guess it's because he's my cousin, you know, close in age and all that." He paused, staring at the ceiling. "Barclays is a huge bank. You say you work at Barclays and everyone's eyebrows go up."

" So," Susan asked mischievously, "you want your share of eyebrows?"

"One or two going up every now and then would be nice." Susan sat up in bed to turn on the lights.

"Hey, what are you doing?" exclaimed David, shielding his eyes with his hand."

"I'm surprised at you."

"What are you talking about?"

"Didn't you come home tonight telling me about the success of your student?'

"Yeah, so?"

"Don't you see," Susan's voice took on a sense of urgency. "Benjamin is beginning to like reading, to like books. Isn't that impressive?"

"I guess."

"David, don't talk like that. It's quite possible his life was changed today. I bet his parents are so glad. Don't you think so?" David thought for a few seconds before slightly nodding his head.

"Maybe...I don't know. I never really hear from them. The mother's remarried. Never met the real father."

"—Meanwhile," Susan interrupted, "I think you should go to dinner tomorrow night and find out who your cousin is. He might be very interesting."

David didn't answer, preferring to stare at the ceiling instead. Waiting for a response but not getting it, Susan turned to shut the light.

The house at 220 East 10th St. did not warrant a second glance as you walked by. It was, to the average passerby, a house similar to others in Brooklyn: wooden frame, white in color, with a porch roomy enough for a few people to gather and talk on warm summer evenings. To the right, a passageway extended to the rear where a comfortable backyard was situated, complete with a two car garage and a small swath of grass big enough for barbecues. The house, in fact, was decidedly common and pleasant. To Sammy Cipher, however, it lacked bigness, the kind that spoke of wealth and importance.

Such was the feeling that gnawed at him walking from the synagogue that Friday after Sabbath services. His house did not compare to those on East 12th or not even the ones on 14th, he thought as he turned a corner, spying it in the distance. But the inside, the inside, that is how you really judge a house, he thought, lifting his head a little higher.

He had gone to great lengths to make sure the interior of his house spoke of splendor. Desiring to live in Brooklyn for the proximity to a Jewish community, and real estate being so dear, Sammy had to make do with the best he could find. Once purchased, the house underwent massive renovation in order to bring it to a level of sufficient richness. The best of everything was used: Italian marble, imported wood flooring, and the most expensive crown moldings.

Some in the community had called him a showoff, a *shvitzer*, as day after day, trucks, carrying items for renovation, unloaded in front of the house. But Sammy didn't mind—as long as they knew these were things he could afford. Certainly, his nephew, the banker, would be impressed. For tonight that was enough.

The seating arrangements that night were carefully managed so that Saul Caspit sat directly across from his uncle, a designation reserved for honored guests on the Sabbath. It was well known in the family that Saul was wealthy. Even more so was the story, spoken of with veneration, of how he made his money; how his father died of a stroke when he was a teenager; how he studied intensely and went on to the NYU Stern Business school, graduating first in his class and going on to earn a coveted position at Barclays, eventually rising to senior management. He was a star in the family. But that night, sitting to the right of his distinguished cousin, consciously comparing the myth to the person, David noticed some discomfort on Saul's face with the role the family had given to him.

To David's chagrin, Sammy, once again, introduced him to Saul as "the teacher." Saul smiled warmly and said, "It's good to see you, cousin."

"Same here," David replied, as the two stood in anticipation of the Kiddush, the Friday blessing.

Sammy stood up and raised his glass. Silence prevailed upon the table. He began the Kiddush chant, his deep, sonorous voice filling the room: "Mizmor Le David," *a psalm of King David*, began the chant. Soon, it transitioned into a call and response as Sammy sang a verse and the table repeated it in unison. It was a beautiful tradition, David thought to himself, one he did not value enough.

"Shabbat Shalom!"

"Shabbat Shalom!"

The deep red wine was passed around the table indicating the end of the Kiddush and the beginning of the Sabbath meal.

"Shabbat Shalom!" cried Esther, Sammy's wife, as she approached David, hands extended in a warm embrace followed by a kiss on both cheeks. "Shabbat Shalom," David replied.

He hadn't been at a Friday Sabbath for some time, disdaining it as vacuous religious tradition done more out of duty than any real feeling for God. But now, David began to reexamine this notion, feeling, perhaps, that he had been presumptuous and scornful, including towards the people presently in front of him.

Soon the men took their seats at the table, as the women entered the kitchen to bring out the meal. Sammy was in good spirits, dispensing wine freely and alternately declaring something and then laughing, his booming voice carrying throughout the house.

"So, Saul, it is good to have you here," exclaimed Sammy.

"Thank you for inviting me," replied Saul, bowing his head slightly.

"A toast, gentlemen." Sammy raised his glass. "To continued success, and to our guest, Saul Caspit, who epitomizes that success despite large obstacles."

"L'CHAIM!"

"L'CHAIM," repeated everyone in unison as they raised their glasses. Saul shuffled in his seat, trying to gain a comfortable position in his chair. He then emptied his glass in one swig.

"Where are you living these days," asked David.

"I'm back in Queens."

"No kidding. I teach in Queens."

"Is that so?"

"Yeah…so when did you move back?"

"About six months ago. It was time to be closer to my son." He looked around the table in search of something and said, almost to himself as much as to David, "I've been away too long."

"I didn't know you had a son."

"First marriage…I was too young. She remarried shortly after. I ran away, and have barely been back since. But it's time now." Saul poured himself a large glass of Merlot.

"It must be exciting, all that traveling you get to do for business," offered David

"It was when I was younger; a good way to forget my sorrows." Saul chuckled and drank deeply from his glass. "But certain things you can never put behind you." Intrigued, David was about to venture another question, but was interrupted by the dishes of food emerging from the kitchen.

Immediately, everyone's attention was drawn to the dazzling array of colors and smells emanating from the dishes placed in the center of the table: a whole chicken, golden brown; two varieties of rice dishes, one with almonds and raisins, the other with peas; heaping plates of cabbage stuffed with seasoned rice and vegetable; baskets of delicate dough baked with potato; a spicy meat stew with roasted garlic, tomatoes and herbs; and lentils sautéed with an abundant amount of onions and rice. David spied three loaves of hot challah bread being passed around.

A few minutes more and Esther, pleased by exclamations of delight coming from the table, joined everyone by taking her seat to the right of Sammy. Amid the sounds of people busy with dinner, Saul Caspit ate lightly from his plate.

"*Beteavon*, good appetite!" cried Sammy enthusiastically to the boisterous table as people enjoyed what seemed to be an unlimited amount of food and wine. David took the opportunity to continue the conversation with Saul.

"How is your son?" he asked.

Pain flashed over Saul's face. "I haven't seen him in so long. I'm not even sure he considers me family. He even has a different name…his stepfather's. It's still a major family scandal." He paused. "I'm sure you've heard about it."

"I don't get involved in family gossip," David replied. "Anyway, I'm sorry to hear that. It must've been hell."

Saul nodded slowly and searched the table for the bottle of Merlot. Finding it, he asked Benjamin, Sammy's twenty-year-old son, to pass it over.

Rapidly, he poured the wine, the deep red liquid spilling some on the white tablecloth, such was his speed in filling his glass. "It was for the best, I think," offered Saul. "We were giving each other too much pain." For the first time, he turned to face David. "It's largely my fault. I worked too many hours, and was always away from home."

"I guess you have to do those things in order to achieve your position," David said.

"Perhaps," he answered, melancholy in his voice and a faraway look in his eyes. "The thing I regret is the effect on my son. That kills me."

Esther approached Saul and asked him about the meal. "Delicious, " he answered, flashing a big smile.

"You said it!" Benjamin replied," "My mom can really cook," he continued, stuffing an oversized piece of challah bread in his mouth.

Soon the plates were cleared to make room for dessert. "Café or tea," called out Esther from the foot of the kitchen.

Conversation had now turned to politics as heaping plates of fruit and mounds of cookies were brought out. David discreetly tugged at his shirt hoping to alleviate the pressure he was beginning to feel.

Satisfied, he reached over for a cookie after deciding there was still room enough in his stomach, now slightly bulging over his belt.

"Those Arabs want us dead," said Sammy. "It's always been like that and it always will... you can't negotiate with Arabs." He reached over for an almond cookie and defiantly popped it into his mouth as if, by that gastronomic gesture, an invitation for violent debate was issued.

"Aba, that is an extreme view," answered his son, Benjamin. "They, like us, are entitled to their own land. And anyway, its widely known among educated Arabs that Israel is here to stay."

"If they know that, why are they still bombing buses and killing women and children?" Sammy popped a grape into his mouth.

"Wouldn't you if you had nothing to live for?" asked Benjamin.

66

"C'mon already with your sympathizing. We pulled out of the Gaza Strip and still they terrorize us."

"I don't think it's that simple," interjected Saul to the surprise of everyone at the table. The other night I saw something quite interesting." Everyone's eyes were fixed on Saul. "It was a documentary," he continued, "on the progression of Jewish settlements in the past thirty years and the pattern of increased confiscation of Palestinian land. That I knew, but what surprised me, even shocked me, was that this accelerated during the various peace processes."

"Yeah, but these settlers, they're being kicked out. We all saw them protesting," replied Sammy as he grabbed a few more grapes from the fruit platter in front of him.

"Those settlements are the most recent with barely any infrastructure in place and, therefore, the easiest to get rid of," Saul explained. "But what is never going to be dismantled are the thriving cities that are on Palestinian land. These are the settlements, the ones guarded by thousands of soldiers who make sure the best water and roads are accessible. Ordinary Arabs look at these cities and say, What negotiations!"

Saul paused, reached for his glass, and shuffled as if to disguise his movement. Sammy grabbed a piece of melon and began to chew violently, a trickle of juice running down the left side of his mouth.

"You start to understand, then, why, in this environment, suicide bombings look appealing," continued Saul.

"They hate the Jews—that's the problem!" declared Sammy, his left cheek bulging with melon. "Anyway, enough about politics; I'm getting a headache. Esther, where's my coffee?"

Saul took a swig from his win glass. Then, he stood up and turned towards the door. "Where are you going?" Sammy inquired, fearful he had insulted his guest.

"Just stepping outside for some fresh air," was the reply he heard as the door closed.

Saul stepped into the clear brisk night, lit a cigarette and surveyed the Brooklyn street in front of him. He wondered at the close proximity of the houses: the people knowing your comings and goings, your marital fights. How can anyone stand it?

Inside, David was trying to find a common thread of conversation among the boisterous participants at the table. It seemed everyone was talking at the same time, vaguely reminding him of a documentary he saw once of stockbrokers in a trading pit. He felt lightheaded, and made his way outside.

Seated on a small wicker couch smoking a Dunhill cigarette, Saul stared out, a glazed expression on his face. "Thought I'd join you out here," David offered, unsure whether his company was wanted.

Saul turned in acknowledgement of David. "Sorry, didn't see you there."

"That's O.K. I'm used to it. I get that sometimes from my students." He chuckled.

"That's right, you're a teacher."

"Yeah, I teach English." David sauntered to the edge of the porch feigning disinterest.

"Noble work."

"That's what they say."

Saul stood up, dragged deeply on his cigarette and walked over to where David stood. He gazed at the row of cars parked in front of the house and exhaled slowly. "Life sure does go by fast," he replied heavily.

He crushed his cigarette on the floor and returned to sit on the wicker couch. "You know, when I was married, I worked so many hours my son would cry when he was alone with me."

David didn't answer.

"A golden cage. That's all it is. "

"You wouldn't think it was that bad by looking at you."

Saul lit another cigarette and then said, "Rarely is a thing only what it appears on the outside. You have to dig deeper to find out the truth." He stood up, adjusted his jacket, and inhaled deeply on his Dunhill.

"So what grade do you teach?" he asked.

"Huh, oh. 6th grade," David replied, a little surprised at the question.

"Do you enjoy it?"

"Yes...yes, I do." He paused for a moment. "I really do. Especially when you've tried hard to reach a student and he finally improves. That's a great feeling. In fact, it happened this week."

For the first time that evening Saul Caspit looked truly pleased. "That means a great deal," he said. "You know," he continued animatedly, "just today my son called me excitedly about how much he's enjoying reading Greek Mythology. You know how that made me feel? It meant more to me, him saying that, hearing him happy, than anything else I've done in the past ten years." Saul was beaming now, his voice elevated in excitement. A passerby looked up towards the porch.

"You know, my son's in the 6th grade. In fact, he goes to school in Queens as well…JHS 157."

"No kidding. That's where I teach English! What's his name?"

"Benjamin, Benjamin Nussbaum."

David looked at Saul in amazement.

If Tom and Mary see themselves as having an immeasurable lot to do with all the things they know and all the things they don't know, and their desire to be just themselves is not seen as fighting with their deeper desire to be all themselves, Tom and Mary will not only be in love, but deeply moving and alive and forming in love.

Eli Siegel

From *SELF AND WORLD: An Explanation of Aesthetic Realism*

The Good Natured Bride

It was two months away from what was supposed to be the happiest day of his life, and yet, Sam Horowitz was miserable.

With each new day he felt it would save so much heartache if he and Sarah Newsome would get married at City Hall. But Sam, with all his inward rebellion, knew he could not go there, for to do so would mean risking many years of silence between him and his parents.

He thought about these things on their way to Brooklyn, where they were invited for dinner at his Uncle Isaac's home.

Sam could no longer refuse invitations to come over for Sabbath dinner, believing that now as he was about to be married, to do so would be an insult his uncle would never forget. So when the invitation came, Sam and Sarah decided to go, especially since she felt it would be good to know future members of the family. But there were a few things to discuss first.

"Sarah, we need to talk," he said with sudden seriousness, surprising his fiancée, who up to that point thought the two of them were enjoying the ride. Sarah turned and looked kindly at him.

"Oh no!" she replied teasingly after looking at him for a few moments, "Will we survive?" Sam shot a glance at Sarah, who had a sweet but mischievous smile on her face.

"Stop joking. This is important," he rejoined, attempting very hard not to show the delight he felt at his future wife's good humor.

"Alright, I'm listening," she replied seriously.

Sam took a deep breath. It was getting very dark outside. Every so often, the light emanating from the street lamps caused a dance of shadows to play out on his face. "I haven't accepted previous invitations from my uncle because dinner at his house always turns into a scene. Naomi, the oldest daughter, hasn't spoken to her father for over ten years." He paused and gazed outside.

"Go on. I'm listening."

"I think she's determined to show how much she hates him. It affects the whole family and sometimes it gets so bad that the police have to be called." Sam stopped, waiting for any reaction Sarah might have. "I just thought you should know that," he continued, "since you're meeting them for the first time and…in case anything happens."

The red light brought their Jeep Cherokee to a stop. To the right, a middle-aged couple walked hand in hand down the dimly lit street. In the distance, a dog barked.

Sam turned to look at his future wife. The worst she could say, he thought to himself as they turned a corner on the way to his uncle's home, is that we'll see them this once and never have to see them again. That he could deal with.

But her gaze was diverted elsewhere, not for lack of attention but for her attraction to beauty that had first captivated him.

"Have you ever noticed how trees look in the evening?"

"Huh? What did you say?"

"Trees... they look so lovely on a clear moonlit night. So mysterious...and dignified. Have you ever noticed that?"

"Not really," Sam replied, surprised at the direction of the conversation. "What do you think about what I just told you?"

After a few moments Sarah turned and looked at him affectionately. "Don't worry," she replied, lifting her hand to tenderly stroke the back of his head. "Whatever happens, keep in mind that they're just people...like us." She smiled warmly. "And besides," she continued, "you know I'm tough; it's one of the reasons you want to marry me."

It was now Sam's turn to smile, both from a sense of relief and Sarah's good humor. He looked at her, and felt that warm feeling of joy one gets when a good friend is around.

As they approached the door, Sam's rising apprehension showed on his face. "Look a little happier to be here," Sarah quickly said to him seconds before Isaac Horowitz opened the door.

He was a somber faced man, with eyes that made one stop and notice. "Thank you for inviting me, Mr. Horowitz. I'm glad to be here," Sarah said, stepping into the home after introductions were made.

"It is our pleasure to have you here for the Sabbath," Isaac replied, shaking her hand as he looked intently at her with a friendly but penetrating gaze. Sarah, who was not put off by the extended

73

look Isaac was giving her, returned it with a big smile that radiated good cheer. It was his eyes that she liked. There was something bright and lively to them, in contrast to the solemn expression that distinguished his face.

"Come, meet my family," he said heartily, ushering them in to his home.

"Welcome! Welcome!" Miriam Horowitz, Isaac's wife, called out with arms wide open as she crossed the living room and approached Sarah and Sam. "Oh, I'm so glad you came," she said exuberantly, embracing both of them. "This one here," said Miriam pointing to Sam, "this one here, he never comes. Already, I see you are good for him. Because of you he visits family. Maybe when you get married he will do it more."

"Aww, come on, aunt Miriam. You know I've been busy."

"Busy, shmeesy; don't tell me you don't have time for family; there's always time for family," rejoined Miriam, looking at Sam and wrinkling her face into an expression that attempted to be threatening, but was soon overpowered by the good cheer that was on the verge of bursting out of her.

"Now, now Miriam, don't scold the poor boy. He's barely been here five minutes," interrupted Isaac, gesturing to Sarah and Sam to take the seats on the right of his own at the head of the table.

Sarah felt strangely comfortable as she took her place. She surveyed the family's heavily decorated walls, on which hung tributes to the Jewish religion, recalling ancient times and devout men who gave their lives in the service of a vengeful and mysterious God.

Like an affectionate social scientist, she observed the boisterous family beginning to take their seats at the table, the two boys with their skullcaps on their heads and Bernice, the youngest girl, wearing a long dark skirt. Isaac began the Kiddush, the traditional Friday service, signaling symbolically and to every one present that the Sabbath had begun.

It was a moving experience for Sarah, hearing Isaac sing the Kiddush. Any movement or chattering that was going on stopped completely as he began to sing an exalted, haunting melody that drew everyone's eyes to him, as if right then and there Isaac was the medium between themselves and God above. Isaac himself seemed to be somewhat transformed, his staid countenance giving way to a passionate appeal to the heavens as he chanted, crying out longingly in a way that seemed to speak of much suffering and much hope.

Stirred by what she was hearing, Sarah whispered to Sam about how beautiful this all was. "Oh this, yeah, its nice isn't it?" he whispered back. Playing with the fork in front of him, he forgot to reply "amen" when Isaac recited the last blessing, indicating the end of the ceremony.

Critical of her fiancé's general lack of emotion, Sarah quickly applied a discreet but forceful elbow to his side, producing a loud, "Amen!" from him, which everyone present at the table appreciated greatly, especially Isaac who, startled by the belated outburst of emotion, beamed at Sam like a father seeing his son hit a homerun for the first time.

The first part of the Sabbath completed, the ritual meal was now brought out. As intoxicating aromas delighted everyone with the thoughts of eating, Naomi, Isaacs oldest daughter walked out of her

75

room, crossed the living room, past the table and curtly said "hi" on her way to the kitchen.

For years Naomi was a source of great distress for Isaac. She decided ten years ago, at the age of 12, that she would no longer speak to her father; and despite the many questions as to whether there was some abuse—to which she always said there was none—and appeals from family, Naomi persisted in maintaining a stony silence.

Everyone knew Isaac was not perfect, especially when he first married and Naomi was born. During family gatherings relatives would whisper about the uncontrollable rages Isaac got into, the way he would manhandle his wife and child when they did something that infuriated him. It was business, always business, he later said, that made him nervous and ill at ease.

As a young father and husband, Isaac was selfish, and as time went on he felt this himself, and turned to God for answers that would help him become a better human being. He hoped Judaism, the deep study of the sages, would take away the searing shame he felt for harming his family, and for spending so much time angry at the world.

Miriam herself tried desperately to put aside her anger. At times the rage would consume her, choking the very words coming out of her mouth. Daily routine and looked-for joys of motherhood never made her forget.

There came to be an understanding between husband and wife as Ari, Samuel and Bernice were born, softening the embittered businessman. And the rest of the family saw Isaac's desire to be kinder and respected him for it. But not Naomi, who looked at Isaac with eyes full of fury, and who, during this time, became a haughty young woman waging war with the world itself.

Sarah realized from the troubled expression that flashed on his face as Naomi passed into the kitchen that Isaac was hurt by his daughter. And sitting there at the table with the family she was beginning to know, she felt compassion for the pain they had felt all these years.

"Let us eat!" proclaimed Miriam heartily, coming in from the kitchen with the last dish, and breaking the quiet that had settled on the table. "Before the food gets cold, Sarah, eat! Everyone eat!" And not needing any other encouragement, everyone began to dig into the delicious food that was arrayed generously on the table.

A few minutes into the meal, Naomi walked in and took the seat next to her mother.

"Hi," Sarah said, smiling and extending her hand out across the table in greeting.

"Hi," Naomi curtly replied, grim faced and barely reciprocating the offered handshake.

"This is Sarah, Sam's fiancée," explained Miriam, looking apprehensively at her daughter.

"Oh... nice." Naomi looked at Sarah momentarily with a half smile, as if what she just heard was as trivial a piece of information as that of a new deli opening down the block.

"You ready to enter slavery?" she asked Sarah pointedly.

"Naomi!" rebuked Miriam with a forceful look. "Don't mind her. She has a strange sense of humor," said Miriam nervously to Sarah.

"Aww, I'm just joking. Everybody here takes things so seriously," replied Naomi. She looked around until her eyes fell on Sam. "How you doing, Sam? Haven't seen you in a while." She picked at a piece of lettuce from the salad bowl next to her.

"I've been real busy lately. You know how it is." he replied, a worried look on his face.

Naomi knew these expressions well. She had seen them before and used them to her advantage. They were the ones people had when calamity was around the corner.

It was generally understood that great lengths would be gone to for the sake of avoiding the agonizing turmoil of the past. This was an unsaid, ironclad rule in the Horowitz household, and Naomi exploited it with astonishing skill.

She looked at everyone, contemplating her next move, like a lioness closely watching her prey. It was then Sarah noticed she wasn't touching any of the food.

"How come you're not eating?" she asked, hoping the question would be a good segway into a conversation at the now silent table.

"I can't eat this food. I'm allergic to it," Naomi replied defiantly.

"Naomi has been allergic to many foods since she was a teenager," added Miriam. "The only things she eats are steak, French fries, bagels and cream cheese…and some vegetables. Drinking is no problem. She can drink anything."

"Wow," replied Sarah, visibly affected, "I'm sorry about that."

"Oh, it's no big deal. You get used to it after awhile," rejoined Naomi. "Plus, a lot of food is gross anyway, so why would I want to eat it," she added with a laughing sneer, as she rose from the table and walked into the kitchen to get something. Seconds later she came back holding a bottle of Coke, surprising no one but Sarah, who thought her behavior strange since there were already enough bottles on the table to accommodate the whole neighborhood, let alone the people at the table. Looking around and realizing that everyone accepted this display of eccentricity, Sarah asked, "Naomi, why did you get a new bottle when there are plenty on the table already?"

"I hate drinking from the same bottles as other people. I think it's dirty," she answered. "I don't know how people go around using the same utensils. Even after they've been washed they're still disgusting."

"Naomi has her own set of silverware," said Miriam, not looking up from her dish.

"Yeah, it's crazy!" declared Ari, stabbing his food angrily as he glared at his sister. "Not only does she have her own silverware, but when we go shopping, we have to buy everything double so *poooor* little Naomi can eat. For God's sake, she has her own set of food. It's unbelievable!"

"Shut up!" Naomi yelled, giving Ari a vicious look.

"No! You shut up!" he yelled back, holding his fork in a threatening manner as if poised to stab. "It's because of you we never have enough money to do anything. Why don't you just get out of here! All you do is cause us a lot of grief!"

"Silence!" roared Isaac, pounding his fist on the table. "We will not talk to each other like this on the Sabbath, especially when we have guests."

Naomi and Ari immediately stopped. Both seemed to be on the verge of exploding at one another with an anger, which, to Sarah, seemed like it was festering for years. She realized now what Sam had meant when he said things sometimes got out of hand in this house.

"I apologize for this," Isaac explained, turning to his guests. "They should know better," he continued, glaring at Ari who seemed to want to say something more but decided against it for fear of invoking his father's anger even further. Naomi, rolling her eyes in a disgusted manner, got up and walked into her room, slamming the door behind her. Seconds later, loud music emanating from her room burst the silence that enveloped the table. "Miriam, go tell your daughter to turn it off. She knows we don't listen to music on the Sabbath," implored Isaac heavily.

"Why do you let her get away with it, Papa?" asked Ari, as Miriam walked into Naomi's room, and seconds later the music subsided.

"Lets not talk about this now, Ari. It's the Sabbath, a time for peace and quiet joy. Besides, we have guests. I'm sure they don't want to be burdened with our problems," he replied, affectionately placing his hand on his son's shoulder.

Thinking of an excuse to leave before dessert was served, Sam did not notice the thoughtful expression on Sarah's face as she looked at Isaac.

"Mr. Horowitz, I thought your singing was really beautiful," Sarah exclaimed. "I've never heard that kind of singing before. Where is it from?"

Isaac's face lit up instantly. Even at his lowest point, when nothing else he did gave him a feeling of self respect, singing the

80

Kiddush on the Sabbath would make him feel as if the Creator himself was smiling down at him.

"My father, God rest his soul, taught me how to sing in the tradition of the Spanish Jews," he began to explain. "The style of singing has not changed for hundreds of years, and it is the responsibility of every father to teach this style to his son who in turn teaches it to his own son and so on, so the tradition is never forgotten," said Isaac meditatively, looking fondly at his son Ari. "Tradition is one of the most important aspects of being a Jew. You must maintain the traditions in order for our race to survive in the future, especially when you have children," he continued, speaking with a fervency he did not have all evening. "It is like I've always told you Sam: you have a large responsibility to God, the community, and to your future family to become a devout Jew. Everything you do including the wedding ceremony will reflect how much of a commitment you have to the Creator."

Sam was caught off guard. He didn't expect Isaac to go into what he and Sarah were planning to do for the ceremony, and Sam knew that Isaac was going to try to convince him that a Jewish wedding ceremony is the only true way to get married.

He thought of this and became furious.

Sam still wasn't over the time a rabbi called him at the behest of Isaac, to say that if he didn't have an orthodox ceremony, their marriage would be null and void in the eyes of God. "The nerve of him trying to rehash that subject now, especially when I specifically told him not to say anything," thought Sam to himself, his anger slowly boiling under his skin.

"Now, look here Isaac. I told you—"

81

"Isaac," interrupted Sarah, squeezing Sam's arm as she turned to speak. "I love and respect your nephew because he is trying to be a kinder man. It's the reason I fell in love with him, and the reason I want to marry him now. And I want to spend the rest of my life encouraging him to be the person he wants to be," Sarah said, looking at Isaac intently. "That is the most important thing, not whether we conform to some tradition. Whatever we do on our wedding day, we want to honor that beginning purpose and in the process make sure it has a good effect on everyone, including you, dear uncle."

Sam was moved hearing Sarah speak. He felt a rush of emotion come over him, and for the second time that night was grateful to her.

Sitting there, he realized that what began as a night he dreaded was turning into one he would always remember, for it was on this night that he was certain, more so than he had ever been before, that he wanted to marry Sarah Newsome.

It took some time for Isaac to respond. He was riveted by what Sarah had said, having never heard a woman speak that way about love and marriage. He didn't expect Sarah's sincerity, and he didn't know how to respond to her as she sat smiling at him good-naturedly. Finally, after what seemed a long interval of silence, Isaac decided that the couple before him were young and hot headed and, therefore, needed guidance to do the right thing.

"Believe me, the two of you will have all the happiness in the world when God is the most important thing in your lives. Sarah, I know what you mean when you say kindness...it is love," he continued smugly, "and when you become good Jews the love in your family will grow and—"

Suddenly, they were all startled by loud music bursting out of Naomi's room.

An Unseen Friend

What men feel about fatherhood is hard to ascertain. Most often, only half the picture is described. Yes, they say, it's a great experience.

"When are you gonna have one?" they inquire, patting you heartily on the back.

"I don't know," you reply, unsure of what else to say. "I'm just not sure if I want children."

Uncomfortable silence. Darting glances. You venture a question. "Do you like being a father?"

They look at each other, eyebrows raised. "Yeah, we love it," they reply, shuffling uncomfortably. "Changed our lives…best thing that ever happened to us."

Well, partly they're right. But that's not the whole story.

My son, Owen James Ridgewood III, is a dear addition to my life. He was born early morning in a New York City hospital on what would promise to be a steamy July day. Glancing out the window fifteen stories up, minutes before his head was visible, I remember thinking: how come there are cars on the road? Why are people going about their day as if nothing is happening? Shouldn't everybody be home waiting expectantly for my offspring?

Then, Owen was born. With barely a second to catch my breath, the doctor handed me a reddish pink being, tightly wrapped, and said, "Congratulations, you're a father!"

What did that mean? What do I do now? I looked about me, waiting for someone to come explain that strange thing I had heard much about, but never really experienced—parenthood! I sat in the delivery room with Owen in my arms waiting for the mighty rush of joy. Instead, I felt nervous, a little nauseous, and in need of an ice pack for my hand—my wife has some grip!

Looking at Owen through the glass partition in the neonatal ward later that night, I did feel wonder, the quiet kind; the type you feel looking up at the stars on a clear night. I was glad Owen was here.

My life since Owen's arrival has been very busy. When I am not consumed by the duties of being a dad, I happen to write every now and then.

For a long time now I simply could not—I was just too tired. I thought, at first, I contracted some sort of strange disease. I've learned since through speaking to other fathers, that we share a common ailment known as chronic fatigue: a condition where one is so exhausted by the duties of being a parent that the merest pause in one's activity leads to instantaneous sleep.

It happened one sleep deprived morning, when, concerned with the results of the digestive functions of my offspring, I thought pleasantly of the free time I would enjoy that day. My wife, Laurel, had told me that she planned to take our boy to visit her mother and would be out the whole day.

Happy day! Finally, I had a chance to get some writing done. I walked around that morning humming, anticipating that fortunate time when I could encourage the literary muse out of hiding.

I was the picture of beneficence, asking my wife if I could help her prepare in any way. No task was too great! No job was too insignificant! I immediately went into action, dressing Owen for the upcoming day, happily anticipating my impending freedom.

Sadly, it was not to be. Shortly before Laurel and Owen were to begin their journey, cruel fate intervened and delivered a crushing blow.

The phone rang. Laurel's mother was on the line. I listened intently, suspicious of the sudden communication. As the conversation continued I noticed Laurel's voice diminishing in cheer. I rushed to the living room and saw my wife looking grim as she hung up the phone.

"Laurel, what's the matter?" I asked, trying to sound sweet.

"That was mother; she doesn't feel well and needs to reschedule our get-together."

My heart sank. Owen cooed affectionately, oblivious to the disappointment I felt.

"Well, things happen," I said, turning to Laurel with an attempt at a brave face. She stared at me standing there with Owen in my arms, her eyes darting between the baby and me as if something was wrong.

"There's one more thing."

"What is it?" I asked.

"She wants me to stay with her since she's not feeling well...just for the day."

"Are you serious?" I asked angrily.

"You know she wouldn't ask me if it wasn't an emergency," Laurel explained. "Besides, what do you want me to do, tell her I can't come?"

"You have to go...I know...don't worry...Owen and I will be fine here." I sank into the couch, placed Owen on my knee, and sighed loudly. Laurel seemed uneasy. "Don't worry," I continued, "I'll be fine here. It's no big deal." Her eyes looked over Owen. "It's not you I'm worried about," she said apprehensively. I looked at Owen and realized the cause of her anxiety—his pants were on backwards.

Once Laurel left for her mother's, I decided to take my son out to the park. It was early afternoon. The weather was sunny, and to make the best of the situation, I thought a brisk walk would do us both good.

Yet, as we walked down the street my thoughts were swirling. Was I to have no free time at all? Am I to put aside all my hopes and aspirations until the next decade? Have I turned into something I don't want?

With every block we walked I became more and more gloomy, stuck within my self and oblivious to the world around me.

Suddenly, Owen let out a bright laugh, startling me. I looked down at his carriage and saw him sitting straight up, his hands waving in the air at a large Monarch butterfly dancing gracefully. Owen was captivated, his big blue eyes following the butterfly's every movement.

We reached the park shortly after, and I settled into a comfortable bench that gave us a clear view of the surroundings. Owen was smiling and clapping, delighted to be outside. Suddenly, he pointed to a big weeping willow directly across from where we were sitting. I looked at it briefly, then remarked slowly: "that's a wiiiillllow trrree." Owen looked thoughtful and I felt like a good

87

parent, dutifully teaching his child the basics of language. Satisfied with myself, I returned to surveying the scenery around me, content with a job well done. But Owen would not let this be. He pointed again to the Willow and made a pained sound, one that was insistent.

Something was wrong. I looked at the willow and turned to Owen, "I see it Owen. It's a wiiiillllow." But this time Owen began to cry.

"What is it, buddy? What's the matter?" I pleaded. He pointed again to the large weeping willow across from us. "Owen, I've seen the tree. It's very nice." He pointed to the tree again, crying with an even greater intensity. I sighed heavily, feeling beset by my son's difficulty, and turned once more to the willow. I looked and looked, trying to feign interest in order to satisfy Owen. I turned to him once more, forced a smile, and returned to the tree, hoping this would be the last time.

But, then, I saw something fluttering around the willow, a shape I recognized —it was our monarch butterfly! As it came into full view, I was struck by the vibrant red and yellow colors on its wings. Gracefully it flew, delicately curving space until it landed on Owens's stroller inches away from his face. Fascinated, he leaned over and extended his finger slowly towards one of the monarch's colorful wings, prompting the butterfly to flap away and fly off. Owen gurgled with delight as we followed the monarch's flight until we could see it no longer.

He beamed at me, proud of his observation. I hugged him and said, "Thank you very much, Owen. I really liked seeing that butterfly." He began to clap and we both laughed.

We had a good time that day, one of the best we've shared so far. A half hour later as I sat on the bench watching Owen drift to sleep, a new sense of happiness came over me, a feeling I hadn't experienced before: I felt truly glad to be a father, and excited for the future experiences he and I would share. I turned, surveyed the scenery once more, and took a long, deep breath.

It was dusk now. A warm summer wind was blowing through the park as the sun descended below the horizon. The shadows of the trees around us emerged, indicating the waning day and, with it, our return home.

I entered our home with Owen on my shoulder sleeping peacefully, then walked to his room and held him in my arms for some time before placing him in his bed. The moon, searching for an opening into the bedroom, entered through a space in the uppermost section of the blinds and rested on Owen's forehead. I lingered a few minutes more, inspired by my friend in the crib.

The door faintly creaked as I closed it behind me and headed to the study. I had some thoughts I wanted to get down on paper, maybe even turn into a story. I thought for some time, and then, it came to me:

The truth about fatherhood is hard to ascertain. Most often, only half the picture is described…

The Devil is in the Details

"We have to move, Robert. The kitchen is too small," Sandra James exclaimed as she rummaged through an overhead cabinet.

CLANG!

"Honey, is everything okay in there?" asked Robert James, not taking his eyes off that morning's New York Times.

BANG!

He looked up for a second, disturbed by the sounds of battle coming from the room ten feet away from where he sat. Coffee cup to his right, a fresh newspaper in front of him, and a bowl of Granola Crunch was all of heaven to him, and he was too pleased just then to be annoyed. Devon, his six-year-old son, had begun baseball camp, and the morning seemed to hold promises of quiet reading and meditation.

You see, Robert James fancied himself a writer. True, he had not worked with the word as diligently as he should have, and true, also, that he would daydream more often than write, but still, he was waiting for the muse in the moments of his days as he labored as a computer programmer for the New York City Department of Design and Construction.

So it was that bright summer morning when the Robins outside sang and the leaves rustled in divine conversation that Robert James looked forward to putting pen to paper and forcing inspiration out.

BANG!

"Sweeeeeetheaaaaaart, what is going on in there?"

CLANG!

He had had enough. He put down his paper, and headed to the kitchen.

Standing there, her hands over her head, surrounded by slightly tarnished pots and pans, was his wife Sandra. She turned to him, a look of frustration on her face.

As a social worker for St. Luke's Hospital, Sandra James had no equal. Colleagues would praise her kind attention to the smallest detail concerning the welfare of a new mother or a recently released senior. There was that one time, still spoken of by the obstetricians, where Sandra tracked down a family, newly arrived from the Dominican Republic, to make sure they had the necessary supply of Similac formula and diapers.

But on that morning, Sandra James was in a state.

"Sandra, what's going on?" Robert inquired.

"I can't do anything in this kitchen. Look how small it is." Robert scanned the space before him. He was aware that it comprised approximately five feet. He had looked at it countless times in the over six years they had lived there, and had always felt it met their simple desires. There was no need, he thought, for anything more.

"We've gone over this, sweety. We knew the kitchen was too small when we bought the house. It was the backyard that clinched the deal...remember?" And indeed it was the outdoor space that captured the homebuyers' instinct of Robert and Sandra James on that afternoon when they said yes to the real estate man.

For his part, visions of rapturous hours writing under a young pear tree motivated the prudent Robert into becoming what some in

America regard as the pinnacle of personal development—a homeowner.

Sandra had no such grand notions. She had always wanted a garden to see nature up close as it grew into fresh forms under her caring hand. But six years later, nature had yielded no bounty other than weeds and insects that seemed determined to thwart her at every turn.

For Robert a different kind of battle was waged. The pear tree had yielded fruit every October for the last four years, which made a delicious fruit compote that Devon loved with his breakfast cereal. But this prize was extracted at no small cost, for the lovely pear tree had acquired a tenant, technically known in the eastern United States as *Sciurus carolinenis*.

In the spring and summer months a white tailed squirrel would raise its head out of a jagged hole chewed into the roof of their home at 334 Angela Drive. It was the scampering above their head one morning at 5:15 A.M that alerted them to the existence of the unexpected occupant inside their home.

What battles were waged in defense of his property, only Robert knew, but it is fair to say that he did not emerge the victor, for the white tailed squirrel, dubbed Diablo by Robert, did not yield his domicile easily.

Emboldened by his victories, Diablo came to regard the beloved pear tree as an extension of his property.

Property, you ask? How can it be that one of God's four legged creatures owns property? Isn't that the purview of man and his wizards of finance?

Yes, property, for while he did not have a six and quarter percent mortgage with Wells Fargo, and New York City did not tax him on water usage, Diablo, nonetheless, came to regard a five feet by six feet space of earth as his to care for and protect.

So it followed that whenever Robert James decided to motivate the muse by sitting under our dear pear tree, Diablo prepared to batten down the hatches and let loose the dogs of war.

Alas, inspiration had to be found elsewhere, decided Robert, and so, being the accommodating type, he gave up the pear tree to our enterprising squirrel and searched elsewhere for the creative catalyst he so hoped for. Indeed, it seemed to Robert James that nature was not too willing a partner in his pursuit of fine feeling.

"We have to move," Sandra exclaimed, a haggard look on her face. "I know we agreed that the kitchen was just something we would live with, but this is getting unbearable." She flung a faded, metal saucepan in the sink.

Robert remained silent, unsure of his feelings. Sandra interpreted it as resistance. Quickly, she formulated a strategy. "You know, if we moved we wouldn't have to deal with Señor Rodrigo anymore." Robert's left eye twitched. Sandra's mouth curved slightly upwards.

"C'mon Robert, you can't tell me it doesn't bother you anymore?"

Señor Rodrigo lived directly across at 335 Angela Drive. It was with amusement that Robert first noticed his neighbor sitting on an ornately designed wooden chair as they moved into their new home on that first day. A cigar in his right hand, a white Fedora hat on his head, and a mischievous smile on his face gave him a charm Robert was not used to in his daily interactions with people. To Robert, Señor Rodrigo's presence that first day in the new neighborhood seemed to symbolize a connection to the exotic, the beginning of a journey that would take him to higher levels of awareness.

"Is he going to sit there all day?" his wife asked.

"I kinda like it," Robert replied, waving hello. Senor Rodrigo slowly nodded back.

But exoticism shortly turned into irritation as the ever present Rodrigo was there to greet Robert in the morning as he walked to his car; in the evening when he returned home from work, and when the harried Robert would look out the window, just before turning the alarm on for the night, curious to see if Rodrigo had vacated his throne.

He hadn't.

It was as if he was the caretaker of Angela Drive, a benevolent being in Fedora hat not wanting to rest until all things were at peace.

But that was not how Robert James came to see him. By degrees the air of mystery surrounding Señor Rodrigo gave way to a newfound yearning for privacy, for a place where no one was around and serenity was equivalent to solitude.

"You know it still bothers me," Robert replied. "How can it not—I swear, the man has no life. He just sits there staring. It gives me the creeps."

"We could get a place on Long Island where you wouldn't have to see anyone," Sandra explained. "We've been through this before," she continued. "We have to come to a decision." Robert's eyes darted from the kitchen to Sandra and back again to the kitchen.

Complete privacy. He could get used to that.

Suddenly, visions of hours spent in the garden composing tales of love and death and love again flashed in front of his eyes. Maybe this was the impetus he needed to write; just maybe this could be the thing to catapult him to a higher level of creative awareness, he thought. At any rate, it would get him away from the damnable Rodrigo. He gazed at his wife's agitated face. "I'm not promising anything," he said after a moment, "but why don't you find a good real estate agent and we'll go to some open houses."

"Oh, thank you!" Sandra exclaimed, wrapping her arms around him.

"Are we finished? Can I get back to my newspaper now?"

She smiled at him sweetly, and as Robert returned to his Granola Crunch he had a sense of a new found masculinity.

That Saturday as they drove to an open house in the Nassau section of Long Island, to a newly built development on the eastern tip, Devon James looked up from the book he was reading and asked, "Where are we going, daddy?"

"I told you we were going on an adventure," Sandra replied from the passenger seat.

"Yeah, but what kind of adventure? Are we hunting monsters?"

"Not exactly, son," Robert responded. "The truth is we're looking for a new home."

"What's wrong with our old one?" Devon inquired. His book fell from his lap, revealing its lively title: **A History of Heroes and Monsters by Percy Quackenbush III, PhD**

"Well, your mother…" Sandra flashed him an angry look. "Uh, I mean, your mother and I feel the kitchen is too small. We'd like to find a house where you can do more in a kitchen."

"Do more? You mean like dancing?"

"Uhm, not exactly. More like—"

"Now don't be silly, Devon," Sandra interrupted. "You know perfectly well we don't dance in the kitchen."

"So what will we do?" Devon continued.

"Hush up now," Sandra demanded. "Be a good boy and don't ask so many questions."

Robert glanced at his son in the rearview mirror. He's confused now, but it'll be worth it, he said to himself as they pulled into the New Horizons Housing Development.

"61…62, here it is, 66 Mulberry Lane," Sandra declared. The car had barely come to a stop before she had jumped onto the curb. "Wow, it's really big," she remarked with enthusiasm.

"You sure it's not too big?" he asked, walking towards her holding Devon's hand. Standing three stories high and approximately fifty feet across, the structure was twice the size of their home in Queens. On its front was a façade of brown brick. Either side revealed vinyl siding. A large window jutted out from the center.

"It looks like a Cyclops!" exclaimed Devon pointing upwards. "Nonsense!" Sandra answered. "It's just right." She marched towards the front door. Robert looked at his son and smiled weakly.

The sun was now perched high up in the vast sky. Not one cloud could be seen for miles in any direction, offering whomever was looking from up above an unobstructed view of Robert and Sandra James as they went about purchasing a new home.

"Welcome to New Horizons!" shouted a medium sized woman stepping out of the front door. From Robert's vantage point, she seemed all smiles and weighty eyeliner. Heavy set with thick protruding lips, she was, Robert thought, much older than the make-up and tight fitting blouse led them to believe.

"Is that a monster?" asked Devon.

"Of course not, son. Now be on your best behavior today."

"Yes, daddy."

"Hi, Sheryl. I'm Sandra. We spoke on the phone," said Sandra James extending her hand.

"How do you do?" Sheryl replied. Broad eyes framed by an over fed face gave Robert the vague impression he had interrupted her in the middle of a meal.

"Robert, this is Sheryl Sadow, the real estate agent for New Horizons."

"How do you do?" Sheryl said again. "And who might this little boy be?"

"Devon, answer the nice lady," Sandra demanded. Devon looked up and then slowly stepped behind Robert's legs. "Don't mind Devon," Sandra said, "it's all new to him."

"Oh, I get it all the time," Sheryl explained. "Shall we enter the abode?" Sandra flashed a wide smile and quickly entered the vestibule. Sheryl followed, explaining all the modern amenities New Horizons had to offer. Robert took a step forward but found he could not move. Devon was holding on to his hand tightly.

'What is it, son?" Robert inquired, lowering himself to eye level with Devon.

"I'm scared," Devon whispered.

"Of what?"

"Monsters."

Devon was scared; you could see it on his face. Robert decided to try and understand.

"All right, buddy. I'm here with you. Whatever happens we're in this together." Devon's face relaxed slightly. "What does Professor Quackenbush say we should do?"

Devon lit up, and then eagerly turned the pages of his brightly illustrated book.

"Here it is, daddy:

WHEN CONFRONTED WITH WHAT ONE THINKS IS A MONSTER BE ON YOUR GUARD FOR SLANDEROUS SAYINGS, FOR SURELY IT IS THE FIRST SIGN OF THE MONSTROUS. SO SAYETH RODERICK THE WISE.

Robert paused in thought. He looked at Devon who was smiling.

"What does *slanderous* mean, daddy?"

"Uhm, it's when people lie about other people in order to hurt them."

"So... if we're heroes we don't let them do that. Right, Daddy?" Robert gazed down at his six-year-old son. Somehow, he felt lighter now than he had all morning. "Right. C'mon, let's go in."

"Original woodwork," Sheryl declared as she took Sandra James around the house. "You can't find it anymore." Sandra nodded in approval, filled with a sense of her own wisdom. "Of course, our customers have the most discriminating taste, which shows in the décor of their homes."

"Of course," Sandra agreed.

"Come, let us see the second floor," Sheryl Sadow declared, leading the way as she rose up the ornate staircase. Sandra quickly followed as Robert and Devon slowly brought up the rear.

"Look at this, daddy," Devon said, pointing to fantastic images carved into the balustrade. Robert stepped closer and saw pictures of barely recognizable human faces, distorted to the point that they seemed comical. He scanned them quickly, pausing at a clown-like face with drooping cheeks and bloodshot eyes. "Is he crying, Daddy?"

"I'm not sure," Robert replied, running his finger over the outlines of the wood. "C'mon, let's catch up with Mommy."

They quickly ascended the stairs and found Sheryl and Sandra in the master bedroom. "Of course, the potential of this house has never been realized," the stout real estate woman stated with an air of expertise. She gazed at the small family gathered around her and sniffed. "The community saw that right away."

A look of irritation flashed over Sandra's face. "Really? This house looks pretty good to me," she remarked. "I'm sure it needs some work here and there, but, offhand, I rather like the way it looks."

Sheryl Sadow walked towards the master bath, opening the door for maximum view. "Well, we knew we couldn't expect much from the previous owners. The husband had come into some money on the stock market, which he didn't hang onto for long. After that he was a mess. He seemed to have lost everything, including his marbles," she said, looping her index finger around the right side of her head in mockery.

Devon tugged on Robert's arm. Robert turned and realized his son was mouthing the word *monster*.

Monster? What could Devon possibly mean? He made a mental note to ask him later when they got home.

It was twenty minutes later that Ms. Sadow locked the front door of 66 Mulberry Lane. Sandra's face was turned into a subtle grimace as she walked into the sun.

"You are free to look further around the grounds. You'll find it is *absolutely* perfect for young children to run and play in," Ms. Sadow explained. "You'll see, as many before you have, that New Horizons is the best place on earth to raise a family. It simply is to die for." She let out a high-pitched laugh. "In fact," suddenly, she plunged into her oversized pocketbook, rummaging for something. Seconds later her hand emerged holding a card between index finger and thumb. Within the palm, partially obstructed, was a vial containing a dark red

100

liquid. "Why don't you come to a barbeque? This is the address of the Jones family," she said, extending the small, rectangular card. "A lovely bunch; the father is in hedge funds. It'll give you a chance to meet the neighbors."

Sandra smiled politely. "I don't know. We really should be getting back," she said, turning to Robert for approval. He nodded.

"Oh, you simply must," Sheryl Sadow declared. "You know what—let's walk over together. It's just over the hill there." She stuck her arm into Sandra's arm, dragging her without waiting for a response.

"What do we do now, daddy?"

"Follow, I guess," Robert replied. He took a few steps, and then stopped. Devon wasn't by his side. He turned and saw him buried in the pages **of A History of Heroes and Monsters by Percy Quackenbush III, Ph.D.**

"What are you looking for, Devon?"

"Hiding places... of monsters," he replied, turning the page with a look of great concentration on his face. "Here it is,"

MONSTERS TEND TO HIDE IN PLAIN SIGHT, MINGLING AND MIXING WITH MORTALS. A GOOD SIGN THAT A MONSTER IS AROUND IS THE PRESENCE OF FLATTERY, FOR AN EVIL PURPOSE SURELY LIES BEHIND THE OILY LANGUAGE. SO SAYETH JAMES THE GENEROUS.

"Hmmm," meditated Devon. 'Daddy, isn't flattery when you tell people how good they are because you want something from them?"

"Yes. How did you know?" inquired Robert.

"Ms. Bella told me," replied Devon, looking up with a wide smile. "She's a good teacher...I really like her."

"I'm glad," said Robert, rubbing Devon's head good naturedly, and thinking of how much his son had grown in the last year. "Let's catch up." They sped towards the bizarre couple walking arm in arm in front of them.

The afternoon sun beat down upon them as they walked over the hill and towards 75 Hibiscus drive. As far as Robert could see expensive cars and lawns trimmed with surgical precision created a panorama of metal and green. Every home lay next to every other in complete similarity. As they approached their destination, a sight unlike Robert had ever seen played out in front of them. The sprinkler systems raised their chrome heads in unison and began to shower the green grass in a regular pattern of movements. It was almost hypnotic, Robert thought.

"Here we are," declared Sheryl as she rang the ornate doorbell. "Lovely people... can't wait for you to meet them." Sandra straightened her blouse. Her face tightened.

"Helloooooo, Sheryl. Where have you been, darling?" remarked a tall, thin woman at the door.

"Keeping the community safe...as always," Sheryl replied, kissing her hostess on both cheeks. "These are the prospective buyers of Mulberry," Sheryl explained with a flourish of her arm.

"How do you do?" Ms. Jones inquired, extending her hand towards Sandra.

"I'm well, thank you. This is Robert, my husband."

Ms. Jones looked him over. "How do you do?"

"Hello," Robert replied. Ms. Jones smiled curtly before shifting her gaze to Devon. For a split second her eyes lit up, almost as if she was drinking him up whole through her eyelids. Delicately, wiping the side of her mouth, she spun around and headed to the kitchen directly behind where they stood.

It was a massive enclosure, fit to feed at least fifty people. Situated into the wall was a Viking refrigerator with four enormous compartments, capable, at first glance, of holding enough food for at least six months should there be a siege. Directly across lay a sleek, stainless steel oven upon which an iron pot bubbled contentedly. On the walls hung images of exotic foods not seen in your local supermarket. Strange, thought Sandra, as she scanned the images-- these can't be beef, or pork, or for that matter, even veal. On either side, in a coat of arms formation were large steel knives crossed and battle ready.

A number of men and women stood in the center, some nibbling on hors d' oeuvres, some holding wine glasses filled to the brim with a dark, red liquid. "Come on," encouraged Sheryl, " Let's mingle."

All eyes turned towards them as they entered the open kitchen. It was friendly enough, thought Robert, as he picked up what looked like a shrimp from a passing waiter.

"Robert," Sheryl called out as she approached a slender, tall man with horn-rimmed glasses. "I'd like you to meet Thurston Allenby, the community board president." Thurston Allenby nodded. "Robert and his wife are thinking of buying the Mulberry residence," Sandra explained.

"I'm sure you'll do much more with that house than the previous owners," stated Thurston. "God knows we could use some new blood in this community. He glanced at Sheryl and smirked.

"Indeed!" declared Sheryl, flashing a toothy grin. They both laughed. "Robert here is in technology."

"Interesting," said Thurston Allenby. "I do a good deal of business with hi-tech companies. What's the name of your firm?"

"I work for the N.Y.C Department of Design and Construction," replied Robert.

"Oh..."

Suddenly, Thurston seemed to see someone across the room, and with a quick 'pardon me' headed in their direction. Sheryl made her way to the appetizers lining the kitchen table.

"We'll stay for a few more minutes and go," Robert whispered to Sandra as he popped another shrimp into his mouth.

"Less than that," she replied. "I don't know what it is, but this place gives me the creeps. I miss home already."

"Just another bite, " Robert requested, searching for the waiter with the mini chimichangas .

"Fine, but keep Devon close," she replied.

"No problem; he's right he—"

Robert looked down. Devon wasn't there.

"Where is he, Robert?" Sandra demanded, seconds from becoming panic stricken.

"Just relax—how far could he have gone?" Robert scanned the immediate vicinity. No luck. He stepped out of the crowd to get a better look. He retraced his steps to the front door, wondering whether that would provide a better vantage point.

A slightly open door to the far right suddenly captured his attention. Devon has been known to wander, Robert thought to himself.

Slowly, he headed towards it. He entered and quickly shut the door behind him.

It was pitch dark save for a dim light at the far end of the room. It occurred to Robert that he was standing on top of a staircase since the light seemed below him. Immediately he became aware of human voices murmuring inaudibly. The hair on his head stood up slightly. What on earth is down there, he thought.

Whatever it was, he had to find out if Devon was there. He stepped down, feeling his way in the dark. Suddenly, his foot hit something solid. He ran his hand over it and found to his relief and surprise Devon's familiar head, instantly recognizable from years of holding him on his shoulder.

"Devon," whispered Robert, "Is that you?" He ran his hand over the small face and felt moist cheeks. "Devon, Daddy's here. Don't be afraid."

A voice, barely audible, pleaded, "Daaa—ddy."

"I'm here, buddy. Everything's going to be o.k." He bent down, grabbed his son and placed him over his shoulder. Devon gripped him tightly.

With his left hand, Robert grabbed onto the balustrade for support. He tried hard to balance himself as he felt the wall for the doorknob.

The murmuring had stopped. In its place slurping sounds, desperate and hideous, filled the dark, dank room. Fear rose up within Robert. He struggled against the terror that was on the verge of overpowering him.

Robert clutched desperately at the black space around him. Getting close, he thought, as he felt his hand mistakenly flip a switch.

Suddenly, light flooded the room. The door so desperately sought after was two steps in front of him. Quickly, he dashed up the stairs.

But he had to look back; he had to see.

Shrouded figures, their faces partially hidden, were looking up at him. Instantly, they approached him in unison. Like wild animals after a kill, blood was dripping down their mouths. On the wall behind them was etched a massive five-pointed pentagram.

Robert jumped up the stairs and out the door, doing the best he could to lock it behind him. His arm shook uncontrollably. He spotted Sandra and sprinted towards her.

Seeing Robert approaching her with such speed and Devon hunched over his shoulder, Sandra understood and made her way towards him. With as much speed as they could muster, they headed for the door.

"Now where are you all headed?" asked Sheryl Sadow, stepping between them and the exit. She flashed a grin so wide every one of her teeth could be seen. "The party's just begun."

"Devon's getting tired," explained Sandra. "It's time we headed home."

"I'm sorry, but I can't just let you leave now." Her smile vanished, and all that was left was the face of a killer. "Not when the fun's starting."

Sandra and Robert eyed each other. Suddenly, Robert grabbed Sheryl Sadow by the neck. "Get out of our way!"

A look of mortal terror passed over the rabid real estate woman's face. The lock clicked, the door opened, and they made a run for it.

An hour later, it was twilight as the James family pulled into their driveway.

"It seems almost unbelievable," whispered Sandra.

"I know. It's like a nightmare you just want to forget," replied Robert. He shut the engine off and looked in the rear view mirror. Devon was sleeping. "Do you think he'll be all right? He was really scared."

"I hope so," Sandra replied. "I couldn't stand myself if he was hurt by this in any way." She sighed, and a silent moment passed between husband and wife. "I'm just glad to be home." Robert nodded wearily as he stepped out of the car.

A few minutes later, Robert walked up the front steps with Devon on his shoulder. Sitting in his usual place was Señor Rodrigo. Robert waved, and Rodrigo, in return, tipped his hat.

Epilogue

Jeremiah Jenkins sat back in his wicker chair, a smile on his face as he stared at Sam Westerfield,

"That last story is a good one," Sam said, turning to the descending Florida sun. Half below the horizon, it blazed red and yellow. "Sun sure is beautiful this time of day," he remarked.

"Yes, indeed," replied Jeremiah. "Ain't nothin' like the settin' sun. Gives you the feelin' you can go on forever." Sam looked at his friend intently for a moment, and then nodded his head slowly.

"Seems to me, a body wouldn't want to go on forever," Sam said. "Seems to me, there comes a time when we need to depart this here world for somethin' a little better, somethin'…a little less painful."

Jeremiah filled his lungs with the sweet scent of dusk. He slapped his thigh and said, "Well, my stomach is tellin' me it's near about dinner time. Mabel informed me she'd be cookin' up some of that delicious Cajun stew I love so much. Wattaya say, Sam? In the mood?"

Sam Westerfield didn't answer.

"Suit yerself, then. More for me." said Jeremiah. He sauntered off into the dining hall.

"Dang it, man," Sam exclaimed, suddenly twisting his mechanical wheelchair towards Jeremiah. "You got the appetite of a horse. Wait for me! I'm comin'!"

Acknowledgements

To my wife Helena, whose thoughtful and encouraging criticisms throughout the writing of these stories were invaluable. Thank you, my dear! My warmest thanks to eminent anthropologist and Aesthetic Realism consultant, Dr. Arnold Perey whose many years of guidance and careful reading of an early draft enabled me to be deeper about the craft of writing. And to renowned filmmaker and consultant Ken Kimmelman, whose critical insights helped me be clearer about my purpose—thank you so much!